T0169936

The Woman I Left Behind

a novel
by
KIM JENSEN

Curbstone Press

Printed in Canada on acid-free paper by Best Book / Transcontinental
Cover design and photograph: Susan Shapiro

This book was published with the support
of the Connecticut Commission on Culture
and Tourism, the National Endowment for
the Arts, and donations from many
individuals. We are very grateful for this
support.

Connecticut Commission
on Culture & Tourism

NATIONAL
ENDOWMENT
FOR THE ARTS

Library of Congress Cataloging-in-Publication Data

Jensen, Kim, 1966-
  The woman I left behind / by Kim Jensen.— 1st ed.
     p. cm.
  ISBN 1-931896-22-4 (pbk. : alk. paper)
  1. Palestinian Arabs—Fiction. 2. Young women—Fiction I. Title.

  PS3610.E568W66 2006
  813'.6—dc22

                              2005033843

published by
CURBSTONE PRESS   321 Jackson St. Willimantic, CT 06226
        phone: 860-423-5110   e-mail: info@curbstone.org
                    www.curbstone.org

Author's Note

The Woman I Left Behind *is a work of fiction with imagined characters, situations, and events. Their resemblance to real people and events is, however, not a coincidence. The chapters set in Palestine and Beirut, while fictional, are historically accurate.*

For Z

There are two lives in every life
the one that you live
and the one you remember

And in between
there are stories

There are two histories in every history
One that is openly told
And one that remains a secret forever

And in between there are wounds
And in between there is poetry
And in between there are stories

1
Night of the Mijwiz

There is a small flute that belongs to Palestinian folklore. It is called the mijwiz and it consists of twin pipes fashioned from cane. The mijwiz does not have a wide range of sound; it produces a harsh, repetitious wail. But for Palestinians, the sound of the mijwiz signals a time of rejoicing. It is played in the streets when the bridegroom is brought on horseback to his bride. The villagers gather to clap and dance folkdances to its tune. The town poet arrives, chanting poetry in praise of the groom and his family, the bride and her family. To hear the mijwiz is to begin dancing; it is an invitation to lay down every burden and to be entranced in the spirit of celebration.

It has been ten years since Khalid has heard the wail of the mijwiz.

It has been more than twelve since he has danced with men and women who clasp hands and bang on the earth with their feet.

But Khalid doesn't think much about things like the mijwiz. He's more likely to remember smells. Sometimes the scent of freshly baked bread is too much to bear. Sometimes he remembers a face—his mother's—which comes to him only in black and white. And in dreams he recalls Aunt Salwa who raised him after his parents died. That was back when his name was still Sayeed, not Khalid. But the mijwiz—that's one thing that doesn't occur to him anymore.

His wife Bernie once asked him why he changed his name from Sayeed, which means "happy," to Khalid, which means "eternal." He told her he wanted a name that would be hard for her to say. He told her this with a soft smile—to let her know that he was joking. But the truth was that even after three years she still pronounced his name "Kaleed," completely and annoyingly wrong. The "Kh" sound had been replaced with the easier "K" sound, and the short "i" had been transformed into a long "ee."

For several months after he arrived in California at the end of '82, he couldn't sleep at night. He was waking up at all hours, sitting by the window, chain smoking and muttering. His anxiety would then wake her up. Half-asleep, she'd mumble something like, *Maybe you should* do *something productive...write letters, join an organization....* But for some reason her comments only added fuel to the flames within him. They only increased the emotional distance between them.

He had never been able to explain to her; he had not told her the whole story, which always seemed too long and difficult to tell, because it reached back into childhood and beyond, into places where it was almost impossible to travel.

It was a hot day in mid-June in Tel Zahara, a village on the northern outskirts of Jerusalem. On his way home from school, Sayeed and his friends had stopped at the village well to drink and splash water on their faces. The year was 1974; and the water was refreshing, cool, and clean. *This water still belongs to me,* Sayeed said to himself as the clear liquid trickled down his face, falling onto the dust around his feet. Some of it soaked into his school shirt, changing its starch-white color to gray.

The summer, with its pure dry heat, was well under way. Signs of war and poverty—the rubble of crumbling homes, carcasses of old rusted cars—were openly exposed to the hot afternoon sunlight. All the shops in the village square were closed for the two hottest hours of the day. They wouldn't reopen until the sun had crossed toward the western horizon. The whiteness of direct sunlight on dust and the blank color of cement and sandstone were almost blinding. That afternoon, Sayeed and his friends were planning a game of soccer in a nearby field.

We'll meet in an hour, he said with one hand on his hip. He dipped the other hand into the bucket again, splashing water down his back.

Though Sayeed was only thirteen he seemed older because of his calm, quiet ways. He was never one to be clowning around or causing trouble at school. He'd always been a private child. It was as if he looked at the world through a veil, an opaque shade that he'd deliberately drawn between himself and everyone else. He smiled occasionally, barely twisting the corner of his lips; but no one, not even his aunt, had ever heard him laugh out loud.

He was just about ready to head home to change his school clothes when he heard the sound. As he looked up, he saw them—the soldiers on their daily rounds, driving slowly toward the well. They hung lazily from their jeep. With the guns splayed out in all directions, the vehicle looked, to the schoolboys, like a large mechanical cockroach. In fact, amongst themselves, they called the army jeeps "saraseer," cockroaches. When Sayeed's friends saw the jeep coming, they ran off—in the direction of their different homes calling out, *Yallah....We'll meet later for the game. Sayeed, go home!* Sayeed stayed by the well, with his hands on his hips watching the jeep come closer and closer.

His skin was damp and glistening. Tiny droplets of water clung to his cheekbones and lips. But it was his eyes that bore that burden of anger. They were fierce. In them, there was no trace of fear, just the reflection of pain and outrage that had been suppressed for years.

There are tears behind a face full of defiance. Oceans of salt water careened against the backs of these eyes. But Sayeed, "the happy one," had learned, even at thirteen, to hold this ocean back. He was that strong, standing alone in the deserted square, while the jeep made a slow turn around him. Sayeed held his head up and stood firmly in his place. He knew them well, these soldiers, though not by name. They'd been harassing him for several months now.

And they knew exactly who he was—who his father had been, his grandfather too. They'd been tracking him ever since they'd seen him, in the winter, picking up a stone by the side of the road, and casting it towards them.

Sayeed now waited with his face held up in the sunlight. The jeep circled him three times and came to a standstill not five yards away. Still, he never once lowered his gaze, even as the sun blazed down, even as it burnt a hole in the sturdy wall he'd built behind his eyes to keep the salty waters at bay.

The Red Sea, the Dead Sea, Al Mutawwaset...but the most beautiful of all was the Sea of Galilee—Tabariyah—where al-Messih once walked on water. How beautiful it was, Tabariyah—the way its blue surface reflected the light of our homeland....We used to swim and afterwards the desert heat would dry us.

This is the dreamy way Sayeed's mother used to talk about her early childhood.

Back when the British were here it was better! she'd declare. *That's how I see it now. They sold us out...but at least then you could drive from Jerusalem to Haifa to Beirut and back! At least then we could visit the Sea of Galilee. What a disgrace! We used to pack up and spend two weeks at the sea every summer. At sundown we watched the seagulls drift and glide and hover like a dream across the water. At night under the full moon near our tents we'd cook over a fire and tell stories and sing songs.*

But Sayeed didn't remember any of his mother's stories or songs. He didn't remember his mother's caresses; he felt them as an absence, a loss that could never quite place itself on a map. Like the spaces between fingers on a hand—the way sand slips between—until the hand remains empty. Sometimes Sayeed was heard to say, "My mother used to tell me," but it was always a slip of the tongue, because he didn't remember much at all.

It was Aunt Salwa who filled in the gaps, who told him stories, who told him who his parents were, what they did, the things they used to say. Whenever Sayeed noticed in late afternoon that Aunt Salwa took a break from her work—the olive pickling or rolling of grape leaves—he'd ask her to tell him about the past. He never tired of hearing about his father Hanna's bakery on the square. About how people came a long way, even from the Old City to eat his Easter cakes, sesame cookies, or *hariseh,* a honey-soaked dessert. The bakery was a meeting place for the whole area. People would come in the morning with their trays full of bread dough. For a few pennies, Sayeed's father would put the tray in his wood-burning oven and bake it. While they waited for their fresh bread to come out, they'd sit and drink coffee and discuss the issues of the day.

And you, Salwa would tell Sayeed, *you were such a lovely boy. That black curly hair and those eyes! Your mother, Halima, God rest her soul, used to teach you long poems. You used to memorize and recite them in all the meetings. What a sight you were, at six years old, singing out verses of Al Mutannebi. Don't you remember any of those old poems now, Sayeed? I suppose not, poor thing....*

In the village square, the soldiers had come to a standstill in front of Sayeed. They called out to him, *Hey, little Arab!*

The boy said nothing. He just stared them down with a glare in his eye.

Dirty Arab! Why don't you say hello?

The soldiers waited and watched the boy.

It was seven years after East Jerusalem, including Tel Zahara, had been conquered by the Israel Defense Forces. Already on the hilltops, they had built two settlements— flimsy portable units surrounded by barbed wire. Ancient olive groves, including his grandfather's, had been annihilated in minutes by monstrous bulldozers. Everyone in the village had lost land. Sayeed, even at his young age, seemed aware that the jeers of these soldiers were not a personal attack, but part of a well-calculated plan.

On a sinking island he would soon place his treasure. On a sinking island he would place his dreams. Aunt Salwa with her tough dawn-to-dusk hands, her never-been-married hands, would peel sabr—bright red cactus—and offer the skinned fruit to Sayeed saying, "Eat this, habibi, and be strong. Apple of my eye, Sayeed, son of my beloved brother." In fig season, she fed him soft purpled figs. In almond season—sour green almonds. For seven seasons she had raised her brother's son this way saying, "Eat this and be strong."

Sayeed would only discover several years later in a fit of tears, as the city of Beirut crumbled around him, that it was his aunt who had been the strong one all along, that she was the one who held the spirit of her people in her clean hands, offering a fistful of homemade zaatar—thyme which she had picked from the mountains. But her trick had been to convince Sayeed otherwise. Years of Aunt Salwa's voice in his ears had convinced him that *he* was the tough one, that he would be the one to stand up and be brave.

Filthy Arab! Move, so we can get some water, one of the soldiers barked out to Sayeed. But Sayeed remained stone-faced. He had decided to stand in front of the well until they were gone. So help him God, none of those soldiers would take one drop of village water. And nothing would make him speak, run, leave, or turn his head away. Another soldier from the group joined in saying, *Hey little shithead, where's your Mama?*

At that moment a breeze danced across his hot forehead and the corner of his lips twisted into a smile as he thought, *This water still belongs to me, and so does this wind. No one can steal the wind!*

Tell me about her, Sayeed used to ask his aunt when he was younger, eight or nine. *Tell me everything you know.* And Salwa would tell him how his mother Halima had been one of the most educated girls on this side of Jerusalem. She had finished 12th grade in one of the convents in the Old City. Her favorite subject had been poetry and she was talented at it. Then Salwa would sometimes read poems from Halima's old notebook:

> *From winter stalks of broken wheat*
> *To spring's bloom in the air*
> *There is no blessing quite so sweet*
> *As what memory places there...*

And then Salwa would talk about her brother Hanna, his prodigious sense of humor, the jokes he used to tell with a deadpan expression that would leave people sobbing with laughter. Hanna was an inveterate mimic, and his favorite gags involved getting up and doing perfect impersonations of local personalities.

Sometimes Salwa's eyes still watered when remembering her brother's version of old Saleh, the town miser. She described how her brother would jump from behind the counter and *become* a leaning and bent old Saleh, craggily opening the bakery door. *How much are those little pastries?* Hanna would capture the old man's sputtering voice and quivering finger pointing to the tray of goodies. *I'll just take the one there; give me that nice one in the corner.* Then Hanna skillfully played out Saleh's reluctant hand reaching deep into the pocket, the slow gripping and turning of the coin, the desperate relinquishing of the money to the counter top.

Everyone watching would be in stitches by the end of such episodes.

But his jokes were always in good fun, ya Sayeed, never malicious. Hanna was good at imitating people, why? Because he loved them, that's why.

Although Salwa would often tell the boy about his uncle and parents, the bakery, the lively political discussions, the anecdotes about local scoundrels and scandals, there was one story that she never discussed with her nephew. And it was, of course, the very story that he was always most anxious to hear. But she never was able to give him a full account. She always told him the outline, the essence of the matter, which was that his parents were gone. She knew one day that she would tell him more, but only when she found the right time, the right words, a good reason to bring an old wound into the light of day. She had her dignity too, and a belief that personal suffering should remain hidden, untouched by speech.

But every so often, usually at night, after visitors and neighbors had gone home, after Sayeed had gone to sleep on his cot in the back room, Salwa would stay up alone with images from the past running—with darkness and solitude for fuel. Even in her days of labor—making yogurt, gardening, picking dirt from lentils—buried images would often come back with no warning in lightning spurts.

A soft violet dawn lit the window facing east in Salwa's bedroom. But the gentleness of sunrise was ruined by the sounds of her parents arguing.

I don't care if God himself comes down and tells me to postpone this wedding party, I'm not going to do it, Salwa's mother was saying angrily. *This girl has waited ten years for her wedding. For God's sake let her have just one day, one single day.* Salwa, who was 27 years old, looked out at the green grape leaves suspended near the bedroom window, listening to what she already knew would be her father's response:

Ya Allah, I can't believe you people! They say that any day now there may be a war. Do you want people to say that while they were fighting for the homeland we were dancing and cooking trays of lamb and rice? Ya Allaaah!

But we can keep it small, insisted the mother standing in her kitchen, stirring a pot of coffee. *I already talked to Im Yusuf. She agrees with me. There's no need for it to interfere with anything. Just a small party.*

Ya Farha, my dear wife, the man said slowly as if talking to a small child. *It's not about the size of the wedding. It's not about the price of the wedding. Any time now, in fact any day now, there may be a war. It is not appropriate to hold a wedding in this climate. Enough.*

Salwa could hear the screen door slam, which meant her father had gone out the back door to his fields. She knew better than to get involved in this debate. Even though it was her wedding they were talking about. Even though she had her own opinions on the matter. After she heard her father leave, she slipped out from under the sheets, went to wash her face and get dressed. She was a tall slim woman with long brown hair, which she usually wore tucked under a scarf. She wasn't considered beautiful, but she had warm eyes that made everyone who saw her trust her immediately.

When she was finished dressing in a tidy skirt and blouse, she walked out into the kitchen. Her mother kissed her on the forehead and sighed, *Come have your coffee.* As the older woman poured out a tiny cup of the rich black drink, the creases on her face seemed deeper than usual. When Salwa looked at these lines, she felt that she could read in them the oft-heard words: *Whatever the sky sends down, the earth has to take.*

Believe me, it's not worth fighting over, Yumma. I don't even want a party. Yusuf and I will go to the Bishop in Jerusalem and that's it...it'll be done in an hour. The papers are ready.

Don't be ridiculous, the mother responded, *A girl's wedding day is a big celebration.* Salwa's mother, a plump aging woman who always wore the traditional white head scarf, looked at her daughter and took a slow sip of coffee. *Ya Salwa, marriage is not easy. When things get difficult later, you'll need those happy memories of your wedding day.*

I just want the memory of actually getting married! If we wait until the end of our political troubles, we'll never get married.

Even your father wouldn't agree to that plan. It would be shameful. As if you had something to hide.

If people want to gossip, let them. I don't care.

Salwa spoke like an adult because she was an adult, although as an unmarried woman she was still considered a girl. She'd been working in the bakery already for more than fifteen years and could run the place single-handedly. She was much more organized than her sister-in-law, Halima, who was book-smart but not very efficient with time or money.

Salwa was also good with her brother's son, Sayeed, who had just turned six years old. When he was a toddler his mother would become exasperated, scolding him and yanking him out of the piles of warm cakes and bread. But it was Salwa who had learned how to keep him occupied in the bakery by giving him his own pieces of dough at a table behind the counter. He would play for hours, rolling it out, making animal shapes, talking and singing to himself.

When he was a little older Salwa also taught him how to check the bread. She told him that when the whole bakery smells like heaven, it's time to peek in the oven. Sayeed would dance around the kitchen singing, *It smells better than heaven, Aamti.* Then he'd peek by himself.

Even now it was still Salwa who thought of ways to keep Sayeed happy. She had suggested to her father that he should give him a baby lamb to raise. And so two weeks earlier for his sixth birthday, little Sayeed got a lamb from his grandfather. He called the lamb "Grabby" for the greedy way she sucked milk from a nipple made from a canvas glove. Sayeed sat in the olive grove behind the bakery in the morning—playing and holding earnest conversations with his fuzzy pet.

Lessons in life had taught Salwa to be calm, to work behind the scenes to do what she needed to do. Rather than ruffle her parent's feathers by arguing and fighting, she preferred to just quietly go about the business of "doing her own thing." After she finished her coffee and a small date cake, she told her mother, *I better get going to work now,* and walked out the door. But instead of walking the short distance to her brother's bakery she turned the other way, headed down to the Jerusalem-Ramallah road and waited for the bus to Jerusalem. The sun had barely skimmed the treetops, and she was already seated by the window of the southbound bus. In a few minutes she'd be at the Damascus Gate.

Salwa sat on the bus and stared up at the collection of Jordanian tanks and military encampments along the way. It was in the first days of June, 1967. Out in the stony fields and olive groves she could see some soldiers sitting around drinking their morning coffee and chatting. The sight was not the least bit reassuring. Deep down she didn't believe anything or anyone would help the Palestinians. Of course, she nursed, as everyone did, the private hope that all the refugees could go back to their homes, and that they would have a country of their own. But most of the young men she'd known hadn't impressed her as fighters. Even her own fiancé, Yusuf, a journalist who wrote a fiery column for *Al Quds* every week, was undoubtedly useless with a gun. The Jordanian Army had always been the butt of everyone's bitter jokes.

So she sat and watched the scenery go by like a dream, as if shadows not soldiers were camped along the roadsides. Soon she descended at the Old City, determined to convince Yusuf to have a quick ceremony, tomorrow if possible. It was still early in the morning, so she knew that he—a city dweller, not a villager, would be at home.

She took her time walking through the *souk,* smelling the coffee and spices. On either side of the ancient stone walkways, she passed the peasant women in their bright embroidered dresses who were just beginning to arrive to sell their fruits and vegetables. It was the season for grape leaves, fresh and tender, which people bought by the bag for freezing and pickling. Out of habit, Salwa stooped briefly to inspect the color and size of the leaves, to feel their thickness. Salwa's family had their own mature grapevines; that very afternoon she planned to pick, wash, and pickle a large quantity for her new home.

Now, years later, in the shade of green leaves, Salwa was preparing dinner in the courtyard of the house she had inherited from her mother. She never did have a home of her own. Or children of her own. She was waiting for her nephew Sayeed—the boy she had raised as her own son—to come home from school. He was all she had. Snapping green beans into a pink plastic colander, she looked up through the canopy of grapevines above her. Thinking back to that day in Jerusalem seven years earlier, she recalled a famous line from Gibran's poetry: *Did you sit in afternoons, like me, under the vines...the clusters of fruit hanging like golden chandeliers?* How close she had come to having a lover, a husband, a fulfilling life...

In the center of the Old City, on the eastern edge of the Christian quarter, Salwa climbed a narrow staircase. When she reached the landing at the top of the stairs, she turned around and looked toward the east. From there she could see the beautiful shining dome of the Al Aqsa Mosque. What a sight! It was lovely, shining in the rosy morning light. Little did it matter that she was a Christian; she was attached to that beautiful religious place and to other mosques near her own village. The calls to prayer which echoed five times a day across every hill and valley brought her a sense of peace and tranquility.

She took a deep breath and knocked on the wooden door in front of her. Yusuf, a young man of thirty years, tall and thin, opened the door with a worried look. He said in a rushed tone, *Come inside quick. We're listening to the news.* He gave her an urgent, inquisitive look that asked her, *What are you doing here?* But just as she walked in the door, she could hear his mother's shrill voice call out from inside,

They've hit. They've hit. They've made a surprise attack on Egypt!

She rushed inside to see Yusuf's parents and two younger sisters huddled around the radio. They were listening to the Radio Cairo announcer saying, *We have word that at exactly 7:45 this morning the Zionist enemy began a series of bombing raids on the Egyptian Air Force....A war in the Sinai is underway....*As the announcer continued, Salwa looked around her at the faces of her soon-to-be family. They were stunned. This seemed to be a bad start to a war that could only get worse. She understood that they were all deathly frightened; she realized that she was surrounded on all sides by people who were unarmed, unprepared, and counting on someone else to save them.

Yusuf's old grandfather sat on a cot in the corner. He wore a white headdress and gray *galabiya.* He and his family were not natives of Jerusalem. In the war of '48 they had fled the port town of Jaffa, taking refuge in Old Jerusalem with his unmarried brother. They had never been allowed to return to their stone home by the sea. Salwa went and sat down next to the old man who was holding a strand of rosary beads in both hands. She kissed him on the cheek, *Grandfather, how are you feeling...what do you think about all of this?*

Ya binti, we're a simple people with a simple dream—to return to our homes, God willing.

She walked over to the window and looked out. Within minutes, shopkeepers were already slamming down the metal gates in front of their stores. Women, who had been setting up their wares on large blankets were walking briskly toward the city gates. In no time the streets were practically deserted.

Yusuf's family continued to draw together around the radio, listening to the Egyptian reports about the war. The newscaster announced that things were going well and that the enemy was on the run. Several skirmishes had been won already. But nothing could have been further from the truth. They would only find out months later that all of those reports had been totally fabricated. The truth was that the surprise attack had completely devastated Egypt's Air Force in three hours, just as the Israeli military knew it would. The slaughter was on.

Yusuf pulled Salwa aside finally to speak to her alone.

Why did you come? Yusuf asked, putting his hand on his bride's forearm.

I came to see you, she said. *I needed to talk to you...*

About what? he asked. She said, *It doesn't matter now. I was going to ask you to go to the bishop with me tomorrow. But obviously that's out of the question.*

I think you should go home to your parents right now— in case things get bad here. Jerusalem will soon be burning. *I want to stay with you for a while to see what happens. If things get bad I'll go home,* she said.

I really think you'd be safer in Tel Zahara, he started to respond until she flashed him a look that said, *I'll be fine.* Yusuf had a thin mustache that he caressed whenever he was about to concede a point. Reaching up to smooth down his little band of hair, he said, *Well, I've been wanting to be with you. I only wish we could be alone together.* That was an impossibility, of course; his mother Im Yusuf had already caught them in her all-encompassing gaze. *Come sit for coffee you two,* she said, gesturing them to the table.

Half an hour after they had finished their coffee, they could hear sporadic artillery and mortar fire not too far in the distance. Some back and forth volleys were popping all along the border with Israel. There was an announcement on the radio that the Jordanian Army had officially entered the war. Air-raid sirens began wailing in all quarters. Jets were zooming low overhead, heading from west to east toward Amman.

Salwa could not believe the speed with which all of this was happening. Bombs exploded closer by. It didn't seem to be in the Old City yet, but it definitely sounded as if East Jerusalem and South Jerusalem were coming under fire. It was impossible to tell from which direction. It was just the terrifying sound of gunfire, bombardments, and jets sizzling across the sky.

Yusuf's father sat down next to Salwa and said, *Some people will be leaving their homes again, like in '48. We will not be among them. They will have to kill me before I leave this house. Salwa, you'll have to stay here too for now. It's not safe to go out. I'll go downstairs to Abu Ali and call your father.*

Everyone watched as Abu Yusuf went quickly down to the shop below, where Abu Ali had the only phone in the building. They sat and listened to the explosions, knowing that with all the Jordanian military stationed inside the Old City, they too had become a target. Every once in a while Im Yusuf would say, *Maybe this is it, maybe we'll see Jaffa again.* No one responded. A few minutes later, after a particularly loud blast someone would whisper, *That's getting close.* Their old grandfather was the only one who made no comment, just counted the beads on his rosary, one after the other.

Abu Yusuf soon came back and announced that Salwa's father was angry that she'd come to town without a word to anyone, but of course he was happy to hear that she was safe. *He agreed that you must stay here.*

Holed up in the second-story room, they listened to the fighting not far in the distance. They had no idea yet of the losses. They thought if they stayed inside, the war might not reach them. But as it was, they were soon to be engulfed. Israeli paratroopers would land in the city by the morning and within 24 hours, all of East Jerusalem would be conquered.

This was another war about borders, and when the fighting stopped they'd again be on the wrong side. Yusuf's family home was already slated with scores of others to be razed. It was built on a site that would soon become an enormous plaza for the Wailing Wall. Within a week after Jerusalem's capture there would be a brutal knocking at their door. The demolition crews would give the family five minutes to collect their belongings and get out. Yusuf and his father would refuse to leave and be bulldozed down with the house.

The thin old man on the cot in the corner suddenly broke

his long silence, telling everyone in a shaky voice, *When we go home to Jaffa we'll have to bring some cuttings from the grapevines here. We'll have to take some jasmine cuttings too. And roses. I'm sure my garden is in ruins by now.*

Snapping beans, one by one, Salwa still had to laugh—the quiet kind of laugh that involves just a small exhalation of air through the nose; the kind of laugh where the head tilts back, and the eyes close for a split second. It's a bitter laugh—when nothing's funny but the lips curl upwards anyway on their own. She snapped beans, nodding her head in a knowing gesture. *Whatever the sky sends down, the earth has to take.* Whenever her mother sighed those words, her head had nodded in the same knowing way. Salwa as a child and then later as a young woman would think, *Why, why, why do we have to take it?* Now she knew.

As she waited for her nephew Sayeed to come home from school, she continued to prepare dinner methodically, using her fingernail to clip off the tiny bean stems on both ends, snapping them into inch-long pieces, discarding the scraps in a small bag between her legs. Soon she would fry chopped onions in olive oil with a small amount of meat, just for flavor. Then she'd add the beans, fresh chopped tomatoes, and *bharat,* a mixture of rich spices. This was her solace: the smell of traditional recipes prepared the same way her mother and her grandmother had done it. As a matter of habit, she always cooked enough for at least six people, in case of guests. As a matter of principle, her door was always open for their possible arrival.

Salwa looked up at the wall clock. Sayeed was much later than usual. It was already past 3:00. Normally he came home from school, had a small meal, and then headed out to play with his friends. She was constantly worried about him. She'd told him probably a thousand times not to speak or even look at the Israeli soldiers who patrolled the streets. *They are just looking for an excuse to beat or shoot someone. Don't give them an excuse,* she had warned him, not a thousand but a million times.

It's the sounds you remember when recalling something you would rather forget. The sounds and the smells come first, then the image or words whispered on the inside of your ear. The sound of the door opening. A glass falling and shattering on the ceramic tile. The scent of perfume, or the pungent odor of fruit left too long on a hot day. For Salwa, it was always the sound of sheets flapping in the wind that echoed through her mind just when she thought she had forgotten the past. That sharp wounding noise remained with Salwa in the inner ear, even on windless summer afternoons.

When war broke out, Salwa spent the whole day at Yusuf's family's tiny flat. In the evening they heard on the radio that the fighting had spread to all the villages on the West Bank too, north and south. She panicked, worried about her family, but the radio kept insisting that a victory would soon be theirs. The shelling was so intense, she knew that she had to stay in Jerusalem for the night, maybe longer. After many hours of sitting up with the family, she finally went to lie down in the one sleeping room. Tossing, turning, filled with restless images, listening to the storm of jets passing overhead, she half-slept on a blanket on the floor. It was just after dawn when Salwa was awakened by an abrupt noise.

She sat straight up and opened her eyes with a start. A bed sheet that someone had forgotten outside was flapping against the window. First the sheet made a loud cracking sound. Then it trilled with a rippling clamor. She immediately saw the haunting sight of the white sheet whipping against the glass. At that moment she was more terrified than during the previous day's sirens and bombings. This eerie sudden awakening was ominous. She imagined her mother's face in the window behind the sheet. *I must go home immediately.*

She remembered the ancient army rifle that her father had hanging on his wall, a souvenir from the revolt of the '30s and then '48. She imagined that his having this gun was probably more of a danger than not having it. She knew her father—he would certainly try to use it before giving up his house and town. She jumped up and practically slammed the window where the sheet was still flapping.

It defied common sense to run out now, but she had made up her mind. She went into action, straightened her clothes, and went to tell Yusuf goodbye. He was brooding at his desk to the sporadic sound of an occasional blast in the vicinity. She came in quietly. And without sitting down she leaned over, kissed him, and said, *I'm going to try to get back home now, quick as I can. Goodbye. I'll be fine.* Before he could stop her she ran out of his room and straight out the door. The cool morning air hit her in the face, and she felt, just for that instant, good to be outside.

The streets immediately before her were deserted. She didn't see any other people or soldiers around. Every few minutes, however, the earth shook with deafening explosions that she prayed would stay away. As she made her way toward the Damascus gate, she saw more and more Jordanian soldiers. Then, as she approached the gate, she saw that the soldiers there were actually engaged in a battle. She had to argue with two of them who didn't want to let her through. She told them that she had to go home to her family in her village. They scoffed at her and told her that she'd never make it alive, but they finally let her pass.

As soon as she got outside, she couldn't believe what she saw. Jordanian soldiers' bodies were scattered about. Right by the Eastern Gate was a civilian bus charred by a bomb and the people strewn like debris, all dead. Could this be true? How could so many people have been killed in one day of fighting? Right down the road she could see several Israeli tanks firing straight at the walls of the city and jeeps moving rapidly toward the Old City. She ducked out of sight of the oncoming troops and ran up a side street that seemed safer.

Seeing that it would be impossible to go on the main Ramallah road, she decided to go the back way, over the mountains, toward her home. Skirting the city wall, heading northwest, she went through the suburbs of North Jerusalem—all of it was already occupied. Not one Arab soldier was to be seen.

Soon she was in the hills, walking along the goat paths that she knew well. When she looked down toward the main road below, she saw a whole battalion of Jordanians scattered along the road. Some of their vehicles were still burning and smoking. They had obviously been attacked from above. Her heart sank, and she began to run as fast as possible toward Tel Zahara, over stones and rocks. What would she find when she got there? Fear and nausea grabbed at her stomach and throat as she ran toward her village.

As she came down one of the last hillsides, she spotted a small flock of sheep grazing without their shepherd. The animals, white and newly shorn, were alone on the mountain, some grazing or bleating, some wandering in circles. It was a scene that she would never forget, the sight of that flock of sheep lost above the road strewn with bleeding corpses.

When she finally reached the hill next to her own village she looked down at the houses in the dim light. The sight that greeted her brought her to her knees. Tel Zahara was surrounded by several tanks, jeeps, and soldiers on foot— she couldn't see everything, but it was a siege. She had never imagined such a swift and terrible defeat. It seemed that not only was her village coming under fire, but the Israelis were firing from Tel Zahara on Arab units across the way.

She quickly calculated who was armed in the village, possibly three or four homes. Some of the older men, including her father, still had old rifles and some ammunition left over from the British days. A few of the young men had joined the Jordanian military, but were not present. She knew that the Jordanian soldiers who were supposed to protect them were mostly lying dead on the roadside. She wanted to run down and tell her neighbors to surrender because she could see from this hill that the situation was impossible.

Crouching behind a rock, she watched and listened. There was an exchange of gunfire. Then silence. Then more gunfire and screaming. A few small explosions and some smoke rising from somewhere inside the village. She couldn't make out what was being screamed, but it seemed desperate and frenzied. After several minutes, she heard a harsh voice shouting, as if commands were being given. Tanks and jeeps started moving quickly into the village. From where she crouched she could see that the Israelis were going street by street, shooting their rifles down alleys, into homes. She watched them moving their vehicles quickly into the square.

It's then that she broke into a run, heading down, darting behind shrubs, rocks, and olive trees. By some miraculous stroke of luck, no one seemed to notice her scrambling down the hill, taking cover when she could. When she reached the edge of her neighbor, Im Azme's, paddock, she hopped the stone wall, went around the house, and ran down a small alley. Slipping in the back door of her own house, she immediately saw her brother Hanna and her father standing by the front window, both with old rifles in hand, taking potshots out the window. She ran into the back bedroom and found her mother, her sister-in-law, and Sayeed huddled behind some furniture. She collapsed on top of them hugging them all, especially her nephew.

Baba, she called out to her father, *Throw the guns out the door and surrender. I saw the Jordanians dead on the road. It's a failure. A complete failure. There is no army coming. You've got to surrender before they burn this village to the ground.*

As if glued to whatever destiny would hand him, Sayeed had somehow come to understand, without planning or thinking about it, that this day by the well would be decisive. There would be no in-between for him anymore. No running, like his friends, who scattered like chaff in the wind, at the sight of the army. He had never consciously planned to stand up to them. But for some reason he didn't have it in him any more to act fearful of soldiers, whose smell alone filled him with disgust.

The soldiers made a move to surround Sayeed, who still refused to budge. One of them was a young Polish kid. He took a step toward Sayeed and looked down into his face. *So what's wrong with you?* Sayeed still offered no response, but glared out of two angry eyes shaded by a forest of dark brow.

Baba, Salwa begged, *For God's sake! Stop it. Throw down the rifle, it's hopeless. The village is already occupied.* She ran from the bedroom out into the living room. Her father was standing by the window; so was her brother. Pushing the loose corner of his checkered kuffiyeh away from his face, her father lifted the ancient gun, carefully taking aim at something or someone out on the street. Then he fired and ducked back. Within seconds a group of five or six soldiers stormed the door, spraying the room with bullets as they rushed in. Salwa dropped back behind the couch and covered her head. When she lifted her eyes again, she saw her father collapse. Hanna rushed straight toward the soldiers, who grabbed him, holding him at gunpoint while he thrashed about, trying to free himself.

When Halima heard her husband's screams, she rushed out to the living room. She paused at the door. First she saw Hanna being held by three soldiers. Then she looked over and saw her father-in-law dead on the floor. That's when she lost her mind shrieking, *Let him go. Let him go.* Salwa told her to calm down and get back in the room, but the woman was raving, *Leave my husband alone. Don't you dare hurt him.* She rushed at the soldiers, clawing them, battering them with her fists. One of them, an officer, drew a small pistol from his belt, put it to her head and shot twice.

With the same pistol, he made a brusque gesture toward the corner of the house. The soldiers led Hanna to the corner and forced him to kneel down next to the wall. The officer walked over and shot him too, execution style, in the back of the head. Then they all left as quickly as they had come.

In the bedroom, Sayeed was wrapped in his grandmother's arms, behind the bed. He kept whispering to his grandma, *What's happening? I'm scared.* And she pressed her lips against his ear telling him, *Don't worry, darling. Everything's going to be all right. Everything's going to be all right.* But when she heard Salwa calling out in a strange voice that was barely human, *Keep Sayeed in the room, Yumma. Keep Sayeed in the room,* she knew something was wrong. She knew that something terrible had happened. Something horrible and irreversible.

Though the older woman held onto Sayeed as tightly as she could, she couldn't stop him from breaking away from her grip. He ran out and went straight to his mother, whose eyes were still open, staring up at the ceiling. A trickle of blood seeped from her mouth. The minute Sayeed collapsed on his mother's chest, Salwa scooped him into her arms and held onto him tightly. Outside they could hear the sounds of shouting and screaming, tanks rumbling through the narrow streets, and the smell of smoke that lingered for the next thirty years.

The Polish soldier took another step toward Sayeed and in broken Arabic said: *You know there are things you don't understand.*

Sayeed looked at him intently. The soldier continued, *Did*

you know that this well will soon run dry? The soldier paused and went on. *We're pumping all the water through our neighborhoods and then back down to you.* Fish *mai,* he said in Arabic, gesturing by crossing his hands in the air. *No water for you.* Then he paused and looked straight into Sayeed's eyes saying, *So here, drink this.* Turning deliberately, he spat into the bucket that sat on the ground next to the iron pump.

As soon as the soldier spat into the water, Sayeed lashed out. Tears leapt to his eyes as he lunged and grabbed the soldier's head with both hands. Pulling back and forth uncontrollably, he screamed, *I hate you. I hate you,* yanking handfuls of hair out with each convulsion. The skirmish was over as soon as it started. The others immediately surrounded the pair in a swoop, bashing Sayeed on the head with the butts of their guns. Throwing him to the ground, they kicked him a couple of times for good measure. Then without saying a word, they picked him up easily and threw him into their jeep. Three of them restrained him. One pointed a gun into the boy's face. One drove north on the main road.

By this time there were a few neighbors coming out of their homes and shops. Some had witnessed the end of the confrontation and had come running. But they were too late. The jeep was already driving away, raising a cloud of dust behind it. They had seen a few confrontations like this before. They thought, as they ran towards Salwa's house, that the soldiers would take Sayeed in for questioning, rough him up a bit, then release him.

Salwa had stopped cleaning beans now and was sitting with her eyes closed, her head leaned back, her head gone back into lost days and hours. She knew that there was nothing she could do to turn back time.... *A homeland, gone. A brother, a sister, gone....* She didn't stir. She clamped her eyes shut. For once, the beans sat uncooked in front of her on the table. She had held everything together. She had worked the bakery alone for three years, then sold it when her mother died. She had given herself over to the task of *sumood.* Steadfastness. When she heard the news about Yusuf being martyred in Jerusalem with his father, she had given herself over to a vow: never to marry, to remain faithful, not just to him, but to her family and her people, and especially to their city, the city of prayer.

Now she sat with her head back and her eyes clamped shut. Until she heard the voices of the neighbor children calling her name from outside, *Ya Aamti! Ya Salwa! Aunt Salwa!* They rushed into her open door with worried faces. And she knew immediately. She jumped to her feet saying in a hoarse whisper, *Sayeed.*

Instead of driving toward headquarters, the jeep headed straight for the border. It took them less than half an hour to reach Allenby Bridge which led over the River Jordan. It stopped at the edge of the wooden bridge. *Get out,* they ordered Sayeed who remained motionless. He didn't budge, so they shoved him out. As soon as Sayeed was standing alone on the bridge next to them with their machine guns pointed straight at him, there was complete silence. There were no more insults or screaming. The soldiers knew the moment's victory was close. *Start walking,* one of them ordered, *Imshee!* The boy didn't understand what was happening to him. He wasn't sure why they wanted him to walk. He looked at the soldiers with a blank look.

Don't just stand there, one said. *You're going back to King Hussein now. We don't want you here. Yallah! Go!* Sayeed looked across the bridge at the desert in front of him, the river down below, slow and murky. He stared at the muddy green trickle of water below him in a daze. *Jordan. Jordan.* He understood now.

It was still hot, the sun wouldn't be going down for a few hours. Sayeed started walking across the bridge, slowly with an almost swaggering gait. He knew the soldiers were watching him. He wouldn't turn around and cry or beg them to let him go home. He walked with his white shirt open to his chest. Feeling the soldiers' eyes on his back, he decided not to give them the satisfaction of seeing his face.

The quiet whisper of the river beneath him gave him comfort. The wooden boards creaked with each step. It might break him, he knew, to turn around, so he didn't. He walked. And never looked back at the soldiers, not once. Off the bridge past the Jordanian check post, into a new land. No passport. No home and nowhere to go. He never turned his back—just kept walking without stopping for hours. Until dusk, he walked. When finally he stopped to rest by the side of the road, the sun was going down, and he was forced to look west, just to watch it go.

The boy said to himself, *I'll be fine. I'll make it.* He wanted to say, *There was nothing there for me.* But these words wouldn't come.

From where he finally sat on the side of the road, he could see a town in the foothills. Later on he realized it was a refugee camp. In an olive grove not far from the roadside, men were starting to string white lights from one tree to the next, preparing for some kind of party. Sayeed heard men's voices in the twilight, saying, *Here, hold the ladder. Okay...it needs to be a little straighter....*One of the men sang out a line from a recent Fairouz song: *Let the night darken, let the night darken....*The voice was strong and deep, filling the air briefly with a tune so familiar that anyone within earshot could have completed the phrase.

Sayeed found himself whispering the song to himself, *Let the night darken, so our lantern may shine brighter!*

He could tell that they were preparing for a wedding. Soon these people would be singing, dancing, twirling scarves and belts high in the air, rhythmically pounding the dirt with their feet. Chanting out poetry and tunes almost as old as the earth beneath them.

Dusk had settled over the land and each tiny bulb on the wire began to gleam, creating a circle of light against the universe's blackness. Women were whispering and swaying, carrying trays of steaming food down to the clearing. They emerged, half-shadows, with their skirts and voices rustling in the dark. From where he sat, Sayeed strained to hear something, a piece of their gossip, the edge of a humorous tale. But instead, all that was audible was an anonymous murmuring, laughter, and the sound of the mijwiz somewhere in the distance. The night had begun.

In Southern California, Khalid feels like a specter haunting this spotless, silent apartment. Night's questions hover around him—the misgivings, the what-ifs, the shadows of a million unspeakable things. Inward, he finds only the shattered mirror of a past—ten thousand miles away.

Khalid looks anxiously at the sleeping form of his wife Bernie. She has always and only tried to help him. Three years earlier, she agreed with no hesitation to marry him into the country. She then helped him to enroll in college, then university, and supported him in every way possible. He has always been grateful for her generosity and solidarity. But gratitude is not the same as love.

2
California Id

On the other side of town, worlds away from Khalid and Bernie, lived a young woman, Irene. She was a student at a big university overlooking the Pacific Ocean.

The university was said to be a good school. But with all the mirrored buildings, and European sports cars zipping around, it was difficult for her to tell what was good anymore.

Having recently moved from the East Coast, Irene found the scenery in Southern California endlessly foreign. Bizarre shrubbery poked, pointed, shrugged, or gestured as if it had been shaped by the wind or other unseen forces. Flowering vines—called ice plants—leaked over walls, yards, and terraces. Irene saw them as slightly menacing; she felt as if she were trapped in a Dr. Seuss tale that had gone awry and from which there was no escape.

Low-flying F-14s and F-16s seemed to be a permanent feature of this new airspace. Zooming out over the Pacific coast from their desert reservations, they created long foreshadows for those on the ground who were attentive to details.

Up on campus, Irene's classes were more like bank transactions. Students, maneuvering jeeps and drinking beer, wrote their questions onto slips of white paper and placed them in pneumatic tubes at drive-thru windows. The questions would be sucked into the void.

Irene wrote down a question of her own: *Why are we*

here? The pneumatic tube hummed and whirred and this response came back: *You are here to run the machines. Someone has to run the machines.*

Part-time, she was a waitress in a small restaurant near the beach—one of those popular brunch places where mild-mannered couples eat on Sundays. She wore a Little Dutch Girl outfit, complete with white bonnet. The owners of the restaurant would charge her if she burned a Danish. They confiscated her tips if she made a mistake on an order. While they rambled together in Dutch all day long, they forced an English-only policy on the Mexican dishwashers, threatening to dock their pay if they spoke in Spanish.

Still, Irene showed up faithfully every day with her little blue uniform clean and pressed.

Far away, Irene's mother was an extremely gifted socialite in an affluent East Coast suburb; her father was a successful business executive with an international reputation. The two of them in tandem had imparted a treasure trove of advice to Irene and her younger brother over the years, but almost all of it seemed remote and useless to her now.

She often found herself talking to herself.

She didn't know where the words were coming from. On the bus she'd hear herself saying things under her breath like, *Cluttered bangled sneer coming down aisle.* Walking around downtown she found herself whispering, *New season of suffering. I will soon stop breathing.*

She had eyes that didn't work. She had whole senses that hadn't operated in a decade. Meanwhile, oceans became plains and plains became mountains under the gaze of her Hollywood-camera eyes. With its mirrored buildings and attention to surface, Southern California was like the opening of a Hitchcock film—placid and serene and imbued with latent terror.

A tourist from Arizona once chased her down the street saying, *Can I take your picture? You, to me, are THE California Girl!*

Actually, I'm from New Jersey, she said, *but go ahead, fake it.* She crossed the street and posed for the picture in front of a red sports car that did not belong to her. Later she wondered why she had told him she was from New Jersey when she was actually from Pennsylvania.

In her dreams her family was a set of painted balloons, each face flying off and away. She chased them across hills, valleys, whole continents, but they were always hovering beyond her reach.

The sadness was almost unbearable.

Irene's roommates, Chrissy and Kat, thought she was, "like, totally weird." Both were from Malibu and drove BMWs (known as Beemers), and were planning on becoming corporate lawyers. They always pulled up to the full-serve section of the gas station, honking until a worker would come out to help them.

Still, the main thing that united the three roommates was this: they had scored big time—their house was only a block from the beach.

Once when Irene went down for a swim in the ocean, people were saying, *No, don't go in.* Then an older man said, *Shut up. She can if she wants.* She dipped a toe, then went all the way out into the water. But when she saw the sharks, she ran back out again. The older man said, *Oh, don't worry, I'll handle them puppies.* He went and grabbed one of the sharks, wrestled it, and wrapped it over his shoulders. When the same shark came after her, she followed the man's example, wrestling it and wrapping it around her shoulders. Then it grabbed at her breasts, and started biting and chewing them. Then it turned into a man.

Actually there *was* an older man who lived near the girls. He was a high school teacher and a soccer coach from Italy named Stefano. He had converted to Buddhism in the seventies and was always inviting her to go for walks on the beach. Sometimes, just to appease him, she'd go. They'd watch the sunset and he would say things like, *You are plagued by what we call Avidya—disturbed mind—you are overwhelmed by the multiplicity of things. Learn the secret of quietness.*

After the walk, he would press her to go further. *Why not come up to my place? I hardly get any visitors. I won't ask you for anything.* She always resisted, although he was just her type—older, olive skin, long bohemian hair. He would say, *Buddha teaches us that all of life is sorrowful. You must discover the path of enlightenment. Come.* For whatever reason, she wasn't yet ready to follow his wisdom.

At night she would be soaring, flying, gliding over the land, over her old East Coast neighborhood, solitary and free. Then suddenly she'd get caught in a bunch of telephone wires. She'd never worry about the obvious—getting electrocuted; she just wanted so desperately to stop being tangled up. To break free.

One day when she was eating her lunch, her boss approached and looked down his nose at her. He was so white she could see every vein in his face. He said in his European accent, *Irene, I notice your uniform is getting tighter. You were much thinner and prettier when we hired you.* She wasn't a complete fool; she knew that he was so cheap he wanted her to stop eating the restaurant food, which was included in her pay. And yet the insult worked like a charm. She immediately slammed her fork down. Later she went to the bathroom and looked at her sad gray eyes in the mirror saying, *I can't do anything right.*

In her room alone at night she would sometimes listen to waves crashing not too far in the distance. She found herself wondering what it was like to be on a slave ship. To be far from home, bound in the bottom of a boat, floating, captive, on a journey to what might as well have been *nowhere.*

It was on one of these nights that Irene was visited by

her first line of poetry: *Cry all night if you want to. The system can't hear.*

These uninvited words ran through her head for the next several days. *Cry all night if you want to...the system can't hear.*

She finally managed to purge the words from her thoughts by scribbling them on a piece of paper, sealing them in a plastic bottle, and casting it into the sea. Little did she know that the line would soon be replaced with dozens more, each clamoring for attention.

Meanwhile Stefano would sometimes drop by for visits; she managed to put him off by skirting the truth, fudging, inventing bald-faced lies. *I have to study. I have a paper due. I have to go to work.* But she never had the nerve or the presence of mind to tell him to back off entirely. She had always been taught to be polite and friendly, especially to those older than herself. She had not developed the will to resist the overpowering logic and drives of others, especially men.

So Stefano kept coming by and calling. Sometimes Irene actually enjoyed listening to him ramble on about his spiritual theories. *Christians,* he'd say, *need to have miracles—raising the dead, walking on water, healing the sick. The Muslims are much more poetic. The beauty of Mohammed's Koran IS their miracle. Such a masterpiece could only be written by the supreme being... But we Buddhists have no need for miracles. The miracle is now, the present moment, your own breath...Wow...Why don't you come up to my place, we can talk about this some more?*

Occasionally Irene would go to local parties with Chrissy and Kat. But everyone looked alike, sounded alike. There would be a keg in the corner of someone's sandy back yard. The palm trees shimmering in the moonlight had more personality than the people. Cloned shorts and shirts, sandals, blond hair, milling around. It was like Melrose Place without the plot or the intrigue. She would have the exact same conversation with ten people, and then go home.

Okay, I'll come, she finally said to Stefano after he invited her to dinner at his house. *But I can't stay late. I have the early shift tomorrow.* While they walked the short distance to his beachside condo, he said, *I have a Jacuzzi. I hope you'll join me—it's very healing.*

Should I go back and get my bathing suit? she asked.

Oh, no need, it's clothing optional.

As soon as she walked in, he closed the door hastily behind her. Then within seconds he tackled her, brought her down to the floor, humped her, and came in his pants. She jumped up and ran out the door screaming, *Get away! Get away from me!* She had experienced this type of encounter before, and this was the last straw. She raced home as fast as she could, feeling a wave of nausea rising within her.

Irene walked in the door, flustered and out of breath. Chrissy put her hands on her hips when she saw Irene.

I thought you went to dinner at Stefano's? Chrissy raised her eyebrows and raised the ending of her statement to form a question.

I did. We ate fast.

Without pausing to reflect on Irene's red face and watery eyes, her roommate asked, *Well, if you've already eaten do you want to go out with us for some fro-yo?*

Okay, Irene reluctantly agreed and went with them in Chrissy's "beemer" to one of those spanking-clean places near the beach, with pink-and-green neon décor. There were potted palms everywhere and traces of sand on the floor that barefooted beach-goers had brought in between their toes.

Irene contemplated the frozen yogurt flavors, finally selecting low-fat raspberry. She thought to herself, *150 Calories, only 25 from fat. I can handle that.*

I can handle that, she repeated to herself again and again.

At the campus drive-through window, she wrote a carefully phrased question: *Is it through reason or faith that humans can best make sense of their painful existence?* When she slipped it into the tube and pressed the button, the question flew down through a tunnel and into the building. She heard laughter from inside somewhere, but no response.

Later, out on the deck of the beach house, working on her tan, she could hear the soothing sound of the ocean in the background. Just as she started to doze off, the phone rang inside. It was her mother, calling long distance. She was saying, *I've got some bad news about Indigo.*

What's Indigo?

You know Indigo, she was your friend. Don't you remember her?

No, I don't. I don't know anyone by the name of Indigo. But what's the bad news?

She's dead.

Hanging up the phone, Irene went immediately back outside to continue her tanning session, slathering a whole new round of coconut-scented oil on each limb. Just as she was about to doze off again, she woke up with a start, realizing, *it's me. I'm Indigo.*

3
The Promise

A pivotal moment was when Irene met Kathy on a bus ride across town, and they became fast friends. Kathy was an ex-philosophy grad student, a budding punk novelist, and now Irene's mentor.

After meeting Kathy, Irene soon began taking her university studies much more seriously and could no longer avoid the truths they were revealing. When she read Sartre's theory of Bad Faith, she was forced to look at herself in her Dutch Girl costume and ask, *Is this who I want to become?* She quit waiting tables and started working instead as a tutor in the writing lab at school.

Kathy was able to see right away that Irene needed to move on in her life and recommended that she decamp to her own midtown neighborhood. *You've got to get away from the beach scene; it's destroying you.* Irene found a place and moved down the street from her new friend.

Irene saw Kathy as a truly free person—completely outside the mainstream. She had crossed over. She didn't sneak into Macy's to buy lacy bras or a formal dress for a friend's summery wedding. Her standard attire was a pair of black jeans, a leather jacket, and boots.

Irene was receptive to all of her friend's advice and suggestions. They went to bookstores, art films, and poetry readings together. Kathy introduced Irene to Rimbaud and Antonin Artaud, and a literary strain of Marxism known as the Frankfurt School. She also introduced Irene to Jules, a critical-theory professor at the university. *You should take your theory requirements with Jules,* Kathy had told her. *He's pretentious as hell, but has a solid class analysis.*

They were driving to Jules' house now, where Irene had been invited for dinner. Irene had never been to any professor's home before and was excited, though the enthusiasm was tinged with several shades of depression and anxiety. Jules had offered to read and critique her poetry and other writings, and so Irene had—with a nauseating sense of foreboding— dragged along a backpack full of folders.

Now on top of this apprehension, Kathy was pummeling her with questions about her family on the East Coast and her childhood. These were subjects Irene scrupulously tried to avoid, keeping the details at the level of an outline.

Why so reticent? Kathy asked as they pulled up at a stoplight.

I can't think about the past too deeply, Irene said, staring out the passenger window of her friend's car. Finally she rolled down the window to take a breath of air.

The past is where everything of significance is found, Kathy said, glancing into the rearview mirror at the car that had just pulled up behind her.

My childhood is just another story of privilege. Comfort, but no soul. Like an Escher painting. Mathematically perfect, but no emotional warmth. Irene leaned her head out the window and breathed deeply again.

Outside, fog and ocean mist hung up under the city streetlights diffusing an orange glow across the jilted alleys and streets. The Southern California atmosphere was haunted, fertile with the smell of saltwater, jasmine, and clove cigarettes that a group of teens were smoking on the street corner. It was late autumn. Leaves weren't falling, but there was a chill in the air. In Southern California there were no dramatic changes in the seasons, just a subtle shift in mild weather patterns.

Kathy tapped Irene's shoulder. *There's beauty in Escher, a lot of movement.*

Lots of movement. People think they are moving upwards, but they may, in fact, be on a downward spiral. And they don't know the difference.

Why all the sarcasm?

See what happens when you grow up having it all? Irene blurted out. *You feel entitled to even more!* Then she fell silent. *It's a paradox,* she added a moment later. *Like Escher,* she finally mumbled to herself.

As they drove north, the skyline of the city became visible behind them. Although there was a handful of tall buildings, it never seemed like a real city to Irene. New York, Philadelphia, Chicago—those were cities. With old steel and iron bridges clanging with traffic and trains overhead; rows of dilapidated brownstone and brick houses; West Africans selling cheap watches and sunglasses—in real cities there were always the simultaneous elements of predictability and chaos.

But this place was balmy and serene. The palm trees were more prominent than the two-story, World-War-II-era buildings. Gracefully arched with their green fringed leaves on top, these trees signified relaxation and exoticism. Meanwhile the architecture called to mind the innocence of the forties and fifties. "Pearl Harbor" seemed to be inscribed in the spirit of the place; it said, *We are innocent; we are victims.*

The primary economy of the city was bomb-building, yet one would never know it to look at the sculpted gardens, the pink stucco exteriors, the sound of sprinkler systems switching on at dusk.

There was a time when all the world was soft, Irene was thinking to herself as they drove through one of the posh neighborhoods in town. *I was once filled with the idea of The*

Good. But the only time I could maintain these feelings of overwhelming love was when I was in solitude—on springtime walks in the rain, lying in bed with the sunshine at my window, praying for happiness for others who were in pain. Pleasure, sarcasm, derisive humor, cleverness—these could be shared. But love, no. Never.

Why don't you blow off work tonight? Irene asked as Kathy turned onto the freeway. *I'll have a better time with you there. I'm a little nervous.*

Kathy was planning to drop Irene at the professor's house because she had to go to her job as a bartender in a motorcycle bar downtown. She'd been working there for a few years. Writing during the day, bartending at night.

Rent is due, Kathy said...*but I'll come back to pick you up if you want.*

Cool. Thanks for driving me around. I appreciate it. Irene nodded.

Irene now lived in a big broken-down Victorian full of transient students. Transient, because someone was always coming or going. A lover would move in, then out. An out-of-town guest would stay, usually for too long. A friend of a friend would be escaping "a bad situation" and need a place "for a while." Irene was glad that she'd accepted the little corner room that no one else wanted. It was roommate-proof—about the size of a large walk-in closet. Luckily, it had one window overlooking a palm tree and the back alley.

Often the real transients would shuffle down the alley with their shopping carts all hung with rags and bags.

The house was situated on the fringe of what passed in Southern California as counter-culture, far from the glitter of the sports cars on campus. Down the street, lined with purple jacaranda trees, sushi bars and sponge-painted cafés with names like Java the Hut were starting to bloom. There was one alternative record store, a leftist bookstore called October, and a health food co-op run by committed anarchists.

Sometimes the members of her household would conduct meetings in the neighborhood cafés. They would discuss things like, *Can we find an organic solution for the cockroach problem?* or *Who keeps throwing their biodegradable scraps in the trash instead of the compost?* or *Are there any underlying issues with the pot plants in my room?* Irene invariably felt guilty at these meetings because she harbored no desire to compost, cook organically, or make homemade glycerin soap. Irene was interested mainly in the poetry of politics and the politics of poetry. Despite this, she felt a deep affinity for anyone who was making any attempt to defy consumer culture.

Sometimes a few of the roommates would stay up late laying plans for underground actions that hovered somewhere between college pranks and subversive activities—that's when Irene's juices started flowing. Designing cut-and-paste manifestos and staging political art happenings—these were more suited to her temperament. She somehow imagined herself as a cross between Vladimir Mayakovsky and Rosa Luxemburg—with a little Dada thrown in for good measure.

And yet, in truth, Irene seemed to have no inner resilience, just a perpetual flux between states of anxiety and exhilaration. She longed for a mythical kind of wholeness and she was possessed by the demons of experiences about which she could not bring herself to speak—even to Kathy.

Kathy interrupted the silence again. *Anyway…I wanted to hear a story or something about growing up in the suburbs.*

I am telling you, there's nothing to say. The burbs are a black hole—all memory is sucked into the void.

Kathy gave her a stern look and Irene shrugged and rolled her eyes. *Okay, here you go. Here's a tidbit for you.* The expression in Irene's gray eyes was somewhere between terror and irony when she started speaking. *When I was about nine, my parents decided to take my brother and me to a folk music festival. I have no idea what got into them. They are country club people to the core. I have no idea HOW we wound up going to this festival—the place was awash with hippies and other long-haired fringy types.*

Irene looked over at Kathy intently, thought for a second, then continued. *What it boils down to is this: anything, anyone, or anyplace that wasn't like them was fun...anyway my brother and I sat in the grass, and listened to the music. We really had a wonderful time wandering around looking at the craft booths, basking in all the colors, smells, and sounds. I had never seen anything like this in my life. It's the closest I ever came to experiencing a sense of freedom. It was very, very short-lived though.*

Why? Kathy asked. She had pulled up in front of Jules' house and was waiting to hear the end of the story.

I was standing in front of a table filled with buttons of all sorts. They said things like, Give Peace a Chance, Bread not Bombs, U.S. Out of Vietnam—it would have been toward the end of the war. I went to ask Mom for money to buy a button. I remember it was the Bread not Bombs that I wanted. It's the kind of logic makes sense to a child.

When I dragged her back to the table, she turned red. "I thought this was a day for acoustic music," she snarled, straightening her linen suit, "not a gathering of anti-American rabble-rousers." The girl behind the stand was speechless. It was humiliating, but the really terrible thing was that Mom dragged me off, and soon we were all in the car heading home.

You're kidding, right?

No, it's true. I know this type of thing doesn't qualify as torture under the Geneva Convention, but it felt like it back then.

You're right; it doesn't qualify.

But it should, they both said at the same time. They were laughing together when Irene slid out of the car.

Within the past year Irene had become the meticulous student that many professors long for. Intelligent, committed, discerning.

Plus insane. A budding poet. Always sitting in the front row asking confrontational, flirtatious questions.

At least this was the way her professor Jules viewed her. When he opened the door to greet her, he remembered exactly why he had invited her to spend time with him. Her attractive face was fresh and open. She was dressed casually, but in an offhand kind of sexy way. She seemed like the sort of student who was game for just about anything.

Earlier that week, when he was walking across campus, he overheard her talking to a friend. *I am unable to call myself a feminist,* she was saying, *because I am still a slave. I know I'm still a slave.*

These words still rang in the professor's ears. They had a certain appealing melody. He was waiting for just the right moment to remind her of these sentiments, and he hoped the time would come soon.

As he let her in, he held out his arms warmly and pulled her in for a congenial hug. The scent of Italian cologne and Bordeaux wine clung to his cheeks.

I liked the poem you showed me at school, he said as he pulled her inside. *What was that refrain? "A word is a promise, and the sound of it breaking." Very elegant. Did you bring me some work to look at? Maybe we'll read some together after dinner.*

We'll see, Irene said. *That would be great.* Jules showed her into the living room, then left to get her a glass of wine.

Irene found herself walking around the room, inspecting the collection of art on the walls. Several Diego Rivera and Frida Kahlo prints hung side by side, as well as some Eastern calligraphy, and some very strange-looking bright-red abstract pieces. She found herself drawn to a large watercolor in the adjoining dining room, a scene of cactus and stones, with some streaked Arabic script painted to look like barbed wire. Something about the lighting and the traumatized brush strokes was almost haunting.

The professor's wife Sarah came up behind her saying, *It's lovely, isn't it? A friend of mine painted it.*

Very moving. Irene turned and looked at Sarah, who was quite beautiful with deep, sad-looking brown eyes, and a massive halo of black curly hair. To Irene, she looked like some kind of Sephardic queen, self-possessed and mature. Sarah looked into Irene's eyes for such a long moment that she felt a surge of embarrassment.

What do you do, Mrs. Reed? she asked, breaking the silence.

Oh my god, call me Sarah, she said, leaning back on her heels, folding her arms. *I work on humanitarian projects for refugees. I'll tell you about it at dinner if you are interested.* She paused, looking again at Irene, who was nodding and smiling. The way the student wore her blond hair scooped into a loose ponytail...her slim athletic figure in jean-shorts with black tights underneath was very fetching.

Anyway, Jules tells me that you're an aspiring poet.

Irene's shoulder bag, stuffed with papers, felt like lead. She shifted it to her other shoulder, looking at Sarah who offered, *Let me take your books for you, Irene.* She put the bag on an armchair in the living room, where it sat for the rest of the night.

Our projects are focused on Palestinian refugees in Lebanon and the Occupied Territories, Sarah said, once they had all sat down to dinner, which was a rich green-bean-and-lamb stew over flavored rice. *Our organization does a lot of educational programs at the university. If you give me your address, I'll put you on our mailing list.*

Oh, I'd love to go to an event, Irene responded just as she finished swallowing a mouthful. *I took a political science class last semester called Popular Movements and Revolutions, and we discussed the issue of Palestine. I'd like to get involved.*

You should, you should, Sarah nodded her head vigorously, smiling at Irene and sipping a glass of red wine. *There are a number of good student organizations. Plenty to do. We're now launching a campaign in coordination with the General Union of Palestinian Students.*

Irene was surprised that it was she and Sarah who carried the whole conversation during dinner. Jules ate fastidiously while listening to the "girls" talking about everything from art to politics, to, *How did you make this incredible stew?*

During coffee Sarah launched into a detailed account of how she had gotten involved in Middle East politics. *I'm Jewish and from a very conservative family. It just happens that I was invited on a tour of the Holy Land ten years ago. It changed my life.*

How? Why?

I went there expecting to return to my roots. Instead, I was shocked by most of what I saw.

I really don't know enough about it, Irene said, *but it must have been hard for you. On a personal level.*

Actually, it wasn't. We...my people...can't afford to take things so "personally" any more. Sarah gestured a set of quotation marks in the air, letting Irene know the disdain she felt for those who let private anxieties get in the way of important political work. *It's much bigger than me. Or my family. Or you. Or...* she started to say something else, and then stopped and caught her husband's eye.

Irene noticed it. Something had passed between the two of them that Irene didn't understand. Whatever it was, Sarah became uncomfortable for an instant. She overcame the momentary lapse by describing the reason for the big fund-raising campaign—a scholarship program for families who had been victims of the war in Beirut.

As Irene sat at the table listening to more of Sarah's story and commentary, she was fascinated. She couldn't help but flash back to the elaborate dinner parties her parents used to stage in their home. The discussions usually centered on polite neighborhood gossip, lawn-care tips, tax shelters, or idle chatter about someone's outstanding or reprehensible game of golf. Thinking back on those dreaded evenings, Irene was even more eager to be meeting interesting people who were involved in vivid struggles. As she listened to Sarah's tales of her work in the refugee camps of Lebanon, she realized that there were actually adults who lived with a sense of commitment and purpose.

The painting you seem to like, Sarah continued, gesturing toward the watercolor on the wall, *was done by my dear friend, Khalid, who was involved in our refugee project.*

Irene's eyes continued to flicker with interest. She had been absorbing Sarah's stories in a wholehearted and thirsty sort of way, all the while gazing at the painting behind the professor's head, wondering about it.

What do the barbed wire words say? Irene asked. *I guess it's in Arabic.*

All it says is "No, No, No" over and over again.

Sarah noted the interest on Irene's face. *I promise to introduce you to him some time. You can't fail to like him. Passionate, funny, handsome…*

Irene was so captivated by Sarah's narrative that she didn't notice the grimace that crossed the professor's mouth at his wife's glowing description of Khalid.

There was something else Irene failed to notice: something was moving inside of her, and she was moving towards the outskirts of her own future. She saw that there was a parallel world to the one she had known and experienced, and that within the bounds of this same city, co-existed a separate universe populated by sorts of people that she had never even imagined: political refugees and the people who helped them.

People uprooted from war zones suddenly entered her consciousness. People whose writings could look like barbed wire. Strong, beautiful women activists appeared on the scene. Women who cast aside personal qualms in order to work for peace and justice. And men, like Khalid whose art was not just a theoretical, conceptual game, or something to be studied at school, but rather something that seemed to be part of a struggle to survive. There was a disarming dissonance in all of this and it was unquestionably seductive.

But for now it was the professor who still wore the mantle of this exciting new territory. He had somehow maintained his status as the proprietor of the mood that was being generated, although he had barely said a word all evening.

For his part, Jules had seemed rather bemused during dinner and coffee, as if he were presiding over his own private brothel, inwardly trying to decide which woman to take to bed that evening.

When Sarah began clearing the coffee and dessert dishes, Jules finally leaned over to Irene and said in a gravelly voice, *I don't think we'll have time to read your writings tonight. Could you please leave them behind for me?*

His silence during dinner seemed to have been calculated to leave an impression. Hearing the tremor in his voice as he spoke about her poems, at the end of such a stimulating evening, produced in Irene a simultaneous gush of relief, gratitude, and anticipation.

Sure. The word sort of melted out of her mouth.

You have a strong intuition, he continued, leaning close to her ear, *about words...their own natural rhythms, the way they speak to each other. I am very excited about your talent.*

There seemed to be a thread between her ear and an invisible point between her legs. Every time his lips came close she could feel a fire run down the length of the string. When the professor finally got up to his feet to clear a plate and blow out a candle, Irene was a little flustered.

A few minutes later, Kathy was beeping outside. After

giving Sarah a sincerely warm hug goodbye, Irene left a piece of paper on the hall table. On it she had written her name, address, and phone number, with a little smiley face and a heart underneath. The contact info and the smile were for Sarah, the heart was for him.

Irene crossed the lawn and climbed into the little car. Kathy's white face, spiky bleached blond hair, and blood-colored lipstick were glowing in the dashboard light.

How did it go? Kathy asked as soon as Irene slid in. Irene heaved a deep sigh.

The only thing I can say is that Sarah is really cool. And I have a crush on him. Isn't that insane?

As Kathy put the car in gear and drove down the block, a smile came to Irene's face of its own accord. She was filled with a whole range of conflicting, yet pleasurable, feelings. Though Jules hadn't said much all evening, his obvious interest in her had soaked into the pores of her skin. And yet her connection to Sarah was palpable. She felt completely at peace in her presence.

Not insane. Typical. What about Sarah? Kathy said without a trace of sarcasm.

She was wonderful. I can tell we're going to be friends.

A looming contradiction. How will you solve it? Kathy said, lighting a cigarette and slumping down in the driver's seat.

I don't know. Something will happen to make it all clear. She looked at Kathy with a bewildered look, a look that said, *I have no idea what could happen to make it clear.*

Oh, you'll lie to yourself. It's the conventional ticket to happiness. Kathy sank even lower in her seat and was silent. She inhaled another drag from her cigarette. They both were quiet as Kathy exited the highway and drove up a long steady hill past the park, past the old art-deco mansions.

The street they were now driving on was designed to

emulate Hollywood elegance. Neoclassical façades lined the curving street on either side. Wide driveways rambled across lush lawns blooming with azaleas, irises, roses, and bougainvillea.

I understand your reluctance to look toward the past. Kathy finally said. *This place creates a sense that you have no history, no roots, no connection to anything around you.* Kathy was squinting and looking out the side window. *The whole ambiance is meant to create the impression that a person can do anything, be anything, become anything. But it can backfire...a person can equally do nothing, be nothing, become nothing.*

I know, Irene sighed. *California makes me feel empty and useless...but I have to admit, I love it too...the Citizen Kane mystique, warm sunsets on the cliffs....*

You are full of contradictions tonight, Kathy said. They drove the rest of the way home in silence. Irene was busy thinking again. This time she was thinking about Sarah. She was thinking about the stories she had shared about her work with refugees. Sarah's voice echoed in her mind: *If our leaders had even a shred of conscience, they could solve the conflict in one day. So much needless suffering.* With these words in her head, Irene watched on as they passed through the elegant neighborhoods and crossed back into their own moderately artsy side of town.

Back at the professor's house, Jules wished Sarah good night and then secluded himself in his study. As if he were about to commit a lewd act, he locked the door behind him, listening to make sure Sarah was really going to sleep. When the ritual of stealth was complete, he opened Irene's cumbersome bag and took out a stack of papers. Not knowing what he might find, he shuffled through them impatiently. There were term papers, poems, stories, odds and ends of ideas. One title caught his eye: *Voice of Bewilderment: Subversive*

Contemporary American Literature. He began reading it and saw that it was a fairly sophisticated paper analyzing her friend Kathy's fiction, which he had only read in a limited way.

He began reading and was immediately impressed. The ideas in the paper weren't entirely original, he thought, but the writing was quite advanced for an undergrad:

> The kind of work that can be thought of as subversive reveals itself as a sensuous, anonymous matrix, a fluid, feminized space where multiple codes gather to form a vision of an alternate world. A place where the "me" disappears, and the "I" comes and goes. Personality is less important than History; Mastery is less important than Destiny…

He read on, and when he finally finished the whole essay, he had to admit to himself a twinge of jealousy…of her youth, her insight, and the fact that she probably had a brilliant career ahead of her. He knew that he had no reason to feel this way, particularly about a young woman, and yet, the feeling was there. And he knew another thing: he was very much looking forward to seeing Irene again at school, as soon as possible.

The next morning, Irene was lying in bed daydreaming when the phone rang. It was Jules on the other end, inviting her to come to his office after class on the coming Tuesday. *I read some of your stuff after you left last night*, he said. *I'd like to talk with you some more.*

Irene was eager to know if the professor liked her writing. But she didn't dare ask. Being on the low end of the power structure, and conscious of it, she would just have to wait until *he* brought it up. But he kept it enigmatic, saying, *Why don't you swing by my office? We have a lot to talk about.*

When Irene hung up the phone she couldn't think straight. She felt hot and clammy inside. Despite her new friendship with Sarah, she had somehow developed an attraction to him. His position of authority in her own field only complicated her emotions. She felt lost and small, yet also powerful and on the edge of something big.

Since she couldn't study or write or do anything else for that matter, she flung herself into cleaning the house with a fury and a passion her roommates had never before seen. Months of bathtub mold succumbed to her ardent scrubbing. Weeks of recycling, weeding, composting was accomplished in a single day. Cupboards—lined and reorganized. The whole house gleamed under her optimistic elbow grease.

At the end of it all she threw herself down on the couch and reread the opening pages of the Communist Manifesto, which was lying out on the coffee table:

> The history of all hitherto existing society is the history of class struggles.
>
> Freeman and slave, patrician and plebeian, lord and serf, guild-master and journeyman, in a word, oppressor and oppressed, stood in constant opposition to one another...

She took in these words, and positioned herself, yet again, with the second half of each dialectical pair.

That same day Jules and Sarah were expecting Khalid and his wife Bernie for coffee. The professor protested that he wasn't in the mood for company, but deep down he looked forward to the combative aspect of these visits.

It was Sarah who had arranged for Khalid to come to Southern California after the Israeli invasion of Beirut four years earlier. He had been working as a counselor in a youth center, but after three months of daily bombardments, then the Sabra and Shatila massacres, he was on the verge of a nervous breakdown. So she persuaded Bernie, a fellow activist, to marry him into the country. It was supposed to be a green-card marriage, but the two of them soon started sleeping together, so no one was quite sure about their situation, especially Khalid.

When they arrived, Sarah gave Khalid a big hug. Bernie, a short woman with brown hair and a large wide mouth, handed Sarah an enormous tray of Arabic sweets, saying, *Khalid bought this for you. It was his idea.*

You know what we should do? Khalid said as soon as they had all sat down with coffee. He was leaning forward, rubbing his hands together. His mop of black curls shook with every word: *Each Palestinian should just light one fire. All together we could burn every settlement down to the ground. It would be easy—Arabs do most of the menial labor. In one day, we could get every settler out.* He stopped and looked around him, his black eyes gleaming with a devious smile. It was less of an actual plan than a conversational icebreaker.

Jules was not in the mood for these confrontational remarks. *Okay, so you're proposing another Holocaust? That's just great.*

Khalid gave him a sarcastic look, *Absolutely not. The settlers can all leave unharmed and go back where they came from. I don't hate Jews. I just don't want these people stealing my land, and then calling themselves the victims.*

To that the professor replied evenly, *I think the language you choose needs to be more diplomatic. You Palestinians need to repair your image in the West.*

Image? Image? Khalid started to raise his voice. Then, instead of exploding, he stood up and said, *There's nothing wrong with my image. We Palestinians are the best-looking people you'll ever have the good fortune to know. Where would you find eyes like these? Where would you find a face like this?* He smiled and posed in front of them all.

Jules was in a particularly edgy mood that day. He didn't know why, but he felt the irrational urge to pick a fight. *With all your good looks and charm, Khalid, you can't be oblivious to the irony of your situation. You claim to reject the West, but where do you wind up when the going gets tough?*

You see, Jules, that's our national tragedy. I have to justify my very existence every day. But I'm used to it. Still standing, Khalid looked Jules right in the eye adding, *That's what makes me so strong.*

Bernie and Sarah quickly found a way to change the subject, and soon the two of them were talking about a play that was showing in one of the avant-garde theaters in town. They were discussing whether incomprehensible experimentation in art should be considered elitist or revolutionary. Khalid finally sat down again and jumped into the discussion of the play.

So they "push the envelope." What if you were to find out there's nothing even IN the envelope? "Fadi," he added in Arabic, then translated the word: *empty.*

I suspect you may be right, Sarah agreed.

*Actually this production...*Bernie started, but was cut off.

You have to look at the thing in its historical context, Bernie started again.

Khalid rolled his eyes. It was just the sort of small gesture that allowed Jules his reentry. He had been sitting in moody silence ever since Khalid's outburst.

Actually I'd like to tell you, Khalid, there IS no envelope, he proclaimed. Khalid waited with arms crossed. *Because language is simply an abstract set of signifiers, unchained, free-floating. Let me phrase it for you in more poetic terms: a word is a promise and the sound of it breaking. Do you see what I mean by that?*

Jules continued in this vein with few interjections from the others, until Bernie eventually rose to leave, making the excuse of too many composition papers to grade.

After they left, Sarah was clearing up the dishes, and

complaining to her husband, *You've become a stranger. I honestly don't know what you believe in. What has happened to you?*

Jules had nothing to say; instead he went to his study and began thumbing through Irene's work again.

The next day Irene was standing outside Jules' office door when he came gliding down the hall. *I haven't had a chance to read all of your stuff,* he said as they entered the office together. Then he closed the door, pursed his lips and added, *but what I have seen is truly promising.*

He abruptly stepped forward and pulled her up close to him whispering, *Irene. Come here.* She was surprised by his suddenness.

No, she said, pulling back.

Why? he breathed into her hair, kissing her neck. *Don't worry,* he murmured, *Sarah and I have an open marriage. Neither one of us believes in monogamy.* He slipped his warm hand under her shirt, leading her over to his desk, gently pushing her down onto a stack of papers.

Her own poem was open on top of the stack.

At the lover's gate, actions speak louder than words, he recited to her as he began to toy with the bottom of her shirt.

I've been flirting with you, she said, sitting up.

Sshhh. It's fine. Sarah and I have an arrangement, he said and placed his lips on hers. Then he leaned over onto his elbows, putting the rest of his weight on her.

The very moment that Jules kissed Irene, an image painted itself onto the darkness behind her eyes. It was Sarah's face illuminated in a halo of gilt light. Like a saint in an ancient Russian icon, her eyes seemed to know and forgive all. Her face was timeless, ageless, with a beauty that transcended each of her individual features. Long waves of hair rippled down the sides of her face, her lips parted slightly as if she wished to speak.

Irene waited to hear what the figure would say. She longed to hear Sarah's voice, trusting her beauty.

Sarah's lips began to whisper, so that Irene had to physically lean forward to hear her, completely dislodging herself from Jules' embrace.

What's wrong? Jules asked as she sat up and nudged him aside.

He wore a childish expression on his mouth that matched his disheveled hair. Like a toddler who has been deprived of a customary privilege, he looked as though he might begin to pout. Irene gazed blankly at his suddenly diminished stature, and realized how ridiculous the whole situation was.

I've made a mistake, she mumbled as she collected her belongings and walked out the door.

Instead of taking the bus, Irene walked all the way home across four miles of paved canyons and mesas, overpopulated with clutters of apartment complexes, strip malls, and traffic. The horizon was hung with a film of smog, and cars whisked by with mechanical indifference. The only other pedestrian she encountered during the entire walk was an inebriated Vietnam veteran who badgered her with bitter reproaches for several blocks.

Spoiled little idiot, he crowed at her. *Look at you. Look at you. Aren't you the smart one?* he sneered, wrinkling his nose, then wiping some snot with his sleeve. He was leaning down low and raising his head to look towards her, as if he were spiritually but not physically deformed. Just as she passed by him, he straightened up and thrust himself right into her face. *Don't think I don't see through people like you,* he said. She didn't respond, but walked ahead briskly. *I understand you very well,* he trembled, pointing at her with a long dirty finger.

Irene was frightened and scrambled quickly to the other side of the street. He followed her for another block, spewing invective, but as soon as she rounded a corner, he dropped back and left her alone.

Once she was out of his sight, his words began to echo in her ears: *Look at you. Aren't you the smart one?*

Spoiled little idiot, she mumbled to herself, mimicking the man's tone of voice. *Spoiled little idiot,* she repeated again.

He's right, she thought. *In his own way, he's right about me.*

By the time she reached her own street she was thoroughly exhausted. It was mid-afternoon. The sun was unreasonably cheerful, and Irene was filled with a hollow feeling as if she'd been sliced open and gutted with a knife. Her feet were sweating and she was deeply ashamed of what she had almost done with the professor.

There was no excuse, she realized, for how poorly she had behaved—flirting with Jules, allowing him to seduce her, thinking that it would all be okay. It wasn't okay. As she walked down her block, Irene remembered what she had said to Kathy earlier that week in the car. *See what happens when you have it all? You feel entitled to even more.* Entitled to take whatever, whoever, and whenever. The American way.

She felt the irrational urge to call Sarah on the phone just to hear her voice, to ask her some simple questions, such as: *How did you manage to grow up?* But she knew that she could never admit what had happened. Sarah's friendship was the real loss, she knew.

Irene trudged up the sidewalk, past her roommates' failing attempt at an organic vegetable patch. The raggedy plants were struggling, had never really taken hold. She looked at the thin, reticent tomato leaves, the stunted green peppers that clearly would never come to fruition, and it gave her the impression that all of her group of friends, herself included, were swimming against an impossible tide, and that the soil itself was rejecting them.

When she opened the door, she was greeted by the sight

of the immaculate house that she herself had cleaned the day before. The rooms had that sterile, aired-out emptiness that is never comforting, except in the way that it tells you, *your work is done for the day.* She nodded in agreement to the voice that gave her permission to grieve, and went upstairs to her little room and collapsed into the stream of tears that had been waiting for a long time.

4
The Escape

Somewhere between my old life and the new
A wave, red henna, the dark shore

Between night and sunlight
A silhouette, an ocean, and a crossing over

If Irene were to tell the story, she would tell it in one way, with one word. Just a whisper. To hear it once would be enough. Enough to enter us quietly. Enough to fill all the shoreless spaces, and to forget the habits and all the little stories we knew by heart. Enough to forget History—the one they write, the one you write—the illusion that we all write together in reconcilable pieces. But all of that is impossible, now and forever, because Irene lives behind the black and white prison bars of these pages.

So the story must be told in prose—like every other tale.

As time went by, Irene began to know deeply and not just FEEL that she had been living in the center of a poison bubble. She knew that there were treats and favors inside, but there was also a scentless venom hovering everywhere.

Between her reading and studying, and her friendship with Kathy, she had begun to prick the skin of that balloon and was starting to breathe fresher air. The fresh air was called "consciousness," and it had the color of morning sunlight. The world was in a halfway place, like dusk or dawn.

In this fragile fertile moment Irene saw herself as

someone who might be capable—one day—of something, not just *escaping* the poison balloon, but creating something else entirely.

And there was one day that forever changed the direction of her life, a day when the world parted in front of her, saying: *All or nothing.*

It was a bright Friday afternoon in April on the campus perched above the Pacific Ocean. An anti-Apartheid rally was in full swing with scores of young activists delivering speeches on the gym steps. Irene was one of the demonstrators, holding one end of a big bold banner that read: *End Apartheid. Divest Now!* She herself had made this defiant banner by hand, painted in red, yellow, and green, with a black fist raised high and strong.

During the past year, she had become more involved in campus politics. It was simple the way it worked. The more Irene learned about power, the more she was certain that she was on the side of the powerless. The more she learned about war, the more she stood on the side of peace. The more she learned about capitalism and its ruthless pursuit of profit, the more she saw socialism as the only plausible solution.

Irene was holding the banner with Kathy and talking. *I've been reading a collection of Che's letters,* Irene said during a lull in the rally, *and I'm amazed by his transformation. He was a medical doctor before he became a revolutionary. What do you think it takes to do this?*

It takes a sense of vanity.

Vanity? asked Irene.

I don't mean pride vanity. I mean you have to confront death and absurdity in a big way. Kathy's big brown doe-eyes were framed by furrows of shorn hair, now unbleached. She opened her lipsticked mouth to say something else, then stopped because the crowd had broken out into loud chants: *Freeeeee Nelson Mandela! Freeeeee Nelson Mandela!*

It's about ecstatic madness, Kathy called out to Irene above the din of the crowd. She then reminded Irene that she had to leave to go catch a plane to New York. They exchanged goodbyes, and Kathy handed over her end of the banner, and walked off.

The hot southern sun poured down on the crowd of colorful students all chanting, *Free Nelson Mandela.* At this moment, the world seemed small to the students, not large. Words spoken in Johannesburg could be heard in California ten thousand miles away. Words sung in California echoed back to Soweto, Cape Town, and Pretoria. And Irene loved being part of the noise, part of the movement. She sang loudly, wondering what or who was next on the agenda.

At that moment a man in his mid-twenties stepped up and volunteered to hold the other end of the banner that Kathy had left behind. Irene had never seen him at these events before. He had dark olive skin, black curly hair, a slim figure. There was both softness and boldness co-existing in his handsome angular features.

He said hello and looked at her with shining eyes. There seemed to be a burning question mark in them. His face was gentle, but tense, as if he'd been waiting his whole life for something. As soon as he said that first *hello,* she knew, or rather felt—or rather knew without knowing—that she was in the presence of a man who could cause her both immense pain and immense pleasure.

The feeling was instantly and crushingly mutual. It was like Braille to a person who can't read Braille. All the signs are there—visible, clear—but for what? As they introduced themselves, they both felt the tug of burning organs even from nine feet apart. He said his name was Khalid. Immediately a quiver of recognition passed through her.

Oh! I've heard of you! she exclaimed. *Aren't you a friend of Sarah's? Aren't you a painter?*

The noise of the demonstration became suddenly

sidelined. They nudged themselves a little closer to be able to hear each other better.

Not really, he answered, *I just did that one thing for Sarah, as a thank-you for her help. I'm a student.*

Then why haven't I seen you on campus before? Irene asked.

I don't go here. I go to State. Don't have the money to go here, he said with a hint of irony.

I'm sure there's a way for you to get money. Bank robbery? Loans? Get a job?

They both refocused their attention on the speaker up on the podium. He was from the Black Students' Union, a well-known local activist. He was talking about white supremacy: *We don't have Apartheid only in South Africa. We need to eliminate the Apartheid system right here in America!* He slowed his voice down and emphasized the words RIGHT HERE, so that the crowd cheered and clapped. Khalid and Irene clapped along in agreement.

Khalid leaned over and asked Irene, right in her ear: *So, how does it* feel *to be a member of the race that rules the world?*

Irene took his confrontational question as a sign of growing intimacy, a sort of come-on. But it was the kind of pickup line that needed the perfect response. *I don't know,* she smiled back, *how does it* feel *to be a member of the sex that rapes, oppresses, and causes all the wars in the world?* He shook his head and said nothing, but smiled.

The two of them slowly moved closer together, bantering back and forth. The banner between them began to sag. All that was visible was *End* and *Now*. The middle section had slumped into a big wrinkle.

So where are you from? she asked.

I'm a Palestinian.

I know that already, she said, *but that means that you could be from anywhere.* She recalled a recent film she had seen depicting the eviction of Palestinians from their homeland in 1948; she was trying to figure out how he might fit into that picture.

So, what then? she asked. *Are you from the West Bank? Gaza? Jordan?*

Where I'm from is a story that might take years to tell... Do you think you have the time?

I might.

By now, all their efforts at banner holding had fallen by the wayside. He was standing right next to her. Shoulder to shoulder. And it was still too far for her. He reached over to touch her long dangling earrings. They were made of red and yellow beads, done in a Navajo pattern. *I like these*, he said. *They look good on you.* She didn't mind his hand next to her hair at all.

All Irene remembers is this: One minute Khalid was saying, *Oh, you white women don't really trust us dark men...* and the next minute they were in bed together stroking each other, speaking in low whispers. In a hushed voice he was saying, *Of course, I didn't mean what I said.*

They were up for hours in the dark, talking, exchanging stories. She told him of lost days when she was tossed about on everyone else's wind. When her only expertise was at failing. When there was not a friend in sight, except men who wanted to use her. She read him some secret poems that no one had ever seen, and he said, *I feel I've known you since my childhood. Since even before I was born.*

His voice was like a breeze blowing through the desert. The one she had been carrying inside of her for years.

That's how Irene now remembers it, dreams of it, retells it, but the steps in between are lost in her memory.

After the rally was over, they slowly walked across campus together. She asked him if he could give her a ride home, since she didn't have a car. He immediately agreed. And they continued walking, their languid pace matching each other perfectly. Khalid would stop in his tracks every time he had something important to say. Then they'd start walking again. Their shoulders or hips bumped occasionally together, and every time they did—a charge of liquid heat would surge through them both.

All of a sudden, Khalid rushed off and away into the grass. In a gesture of absolute ease, he reached up and plucked a small orange from a nearby tree. He was back by her side in an instant. He held it first to his, then to her, nose. *Breathe deeply*, he said, *smell right here.* He pointed to the small hole where the stem had been pulled out and a tiny bit of pale fruit was visible. *That's the smell of Palestine,* he said. *The citrus groves of my sad homeland...*

Then he peeled the orange and tasted it. *Not bad,* he said, *not bad.* He broke off a soft section for Irene and placed it in her mouth. She thought she could feel him right then and there entering her body.

See? she said brightly as she slid into his car, *if you can afford to drive a car, then you can afford to go to this school.*

How do you know my grades are good enough?

She scoffed. *Any idiot can go here. Have you seen some of the people heckling the demonstration, talking about "constructive engagement" with South Africa?*

"Constructive engagement," Khalid said, *that's the latest way of saying, "Let's do nothing about Apartheid."*

"And make some money while we're at it!" Irene added.

On the ride home, Irene found out that besides politics Khalid liked the arts, especially poetry. *Which poets do you like? What else do you read? What do you think of so and so and so?* became the questions that filled the space between them. Rimbaud, Baudelaire, Dickinson, Rilke, the Dadaists, Mayakovsky, and others were thrown out, discussed, became mutual references. This literary connection worked like magic on Irene. For the very first time in her life she consciously reached over and buckled her seatbelt. For the first time in her life she found herself thinking, *Things are just getting good around here. I don't want to die yet.*

Soon Khalid started talking about Sarah and Jules—their common friends. He obviously didn't think much of the literature professor. *I can't stand that pretentious asshole,* Khalid said, *but I have no choice but to see him sometimes. Sarah is my comrade. Believe it or not, she's actually the one who arranged for me to come here from Beirut.*

Aha! Irene interjected, pouncing on this way to change an uncomfortable subject, *so you're from Beirut!*

Well, it's a longer story than that, he said, *maybe we'll talk about it some time.*

*Well...*she faked a hesitant attitude.

It's too late. You're not going to get away from me now.

They had just pulled up in front of Irene's house. She invited him in for coffee, and there was no way he was going to decline.

He told her as he walked in the door, *You know I stopped for a month in London on my way here. In London when a girl would ask, "Wanna come up fa' coffee" it really meant "Wanna come up for a fuck?"* Irene laughed loudly and said, *They have different customs in London. I personally am dying for a real live cup of coffee.* Irene didn't mind Khalid's bold, straightforward style, in fact she saw him as the first truthful man she had met. She was finally in the company of someone who was unrestrained by rules and conventions, and she liked this for a change.

They went into the kitchen and she seated him at a shabby little wooden table in the corner near the window. Meanwhile she busied herself with making a small pot of coffee for both of them.

You know, she said, once she had put a mug on the table in front of him, *that's not a very good way to seduce me—to mention all of that coffee you've been drinking in London.*

Khalid combed his black curls back with his fingertips. *I didn't say I actually drank the coffee. I just said I was invited.*

Irene pulled a bag of cookies from her backpack, and set them before him on the table. He munched on them happily, dipping them in the coffee and grinning.

So if you aren't a painter, what are you then? she asked.

I'm studying political science, but I write poetry too.

In Arabic or in English?

Both.

Recite something for me.

He closed his eyes and said,

> *My love, you are blue ocean,*
> *light upon waves.*
> *You are the fish and seabirds flying*
> *You are the unknown next,*
> *the joy of songs,*
> *the tears of the unsayable…*

Beautiful, she said, *did you write it?*

I just made it up for you.

With every word spoken between them, he leaned closer into her aura, and she was letting her fingers brush his arm and shoulder when she spoke. *I'd like to build you a shack on the hills of Jerusalem,* he told her, *and we'd raise goats together and read and write poetry all day long.* And she asked, *Could we have a horse too? I've always wanted a horse.*

One minute they were drinking coffee, thick with cream and sugar, and eating broken chocolate chip cookies. The next minute they were up in her tiny room holding each other, his warm hands running up and down her body, their lips making promises and plans. Soon they would climb trees together like children, roll and make love in the grass, and let the purple jacaranda blossoms of springtime fall all over them. At night they would stay up for hours, talking, agreeing that they were soulmates, eternal lovers, and would never be parted.

Palestine is a bleeding wound, he told her. *We've been bleeding for forty years.* He touched his naked rib as if to show her an open gash. He reached out and pulled her on top of him. *Press down on me hard,* he said, *make me disappear.* And she did. She made him disappear, beneath her hair, her kisses, her naked tears driven into the crevices and ravines of his body.

That's the way they both remember it and dream of it and tell it. But it didn't happen just that way. There were other things that came first.

They were still sitting and talking face to face at the kitchen table. He had just recited a long poem by Khalil Gibran by heart. First in Arabic, then in English. *Give me the flute and sing,* he recited. *For singing is the secret of being. And the echo of the flute remains, after existence is gone.*

She loved the sound of the Arabic language and was transported by Gibran's poetry to a world that she hoped actually existed somewhere. A world that did not include banal choices like paper or plastic, Democrats and Republicans, pass or fail. She was already dreaming of that little shack they would have in the hills of Jerusalem, sheltered by grapevines all hung with chandeliers of golden fruit.

Meanwhile Khalid settled back in his chair and was kneading his fist into his palm. His conscience was beginning to bristle.

I need to tell you something, he blurted out in a strange voice, *and I don't want you to take it the wrong way.* They were alone in the old house. None of her roommates had come home yet. Evening was starting to fall over half of the table, an orange light was melting the cracked wooden windowsills across the room. *What?* she asked, worried. *What?* She sat up in her chair, tightening her brows.

I like you a lot, he said, *I'd like to stay here all evening...*

But? Her stomach flipped like a crumpled pancake.

But...you should know...I'm married.

What? You're kidding! She tried to pretend that she wasn't completely destroyed by his revelation. *Married? You're too young to be married!*

It's not a real marriage, he added hastily.

Hmmm...

No, really. It's a Green Card arrangement. A political thing. It's not a real marriage at all. Sarah fixed it up for me.

Then why are you telling me about it?

It's pretty complex. We do live together.

Irene immediately interpreted "we live together" to mean "we sleep together." *What am I supposed to do with this information?* Irene asked.

Now that you know, Khalid looked out innocently behind long thick eyelashes, *I hope you'll ignore it.* This answer took her aback.

That would be easier for me, than for you, obviously.

But don't forget what I just told you, he almost begged. *It's not a real marriage. We never really committed to this thing. It's just been sort of blowing along...blowing along.... There's no love.*

I bet you wouldn't say that if she were here.

She knows it already. We both know it.

Excuse me, Irene said, *but I need to go to the bathroom.* She shoved her chair back and walked briskly out of the room. While she was gone, Khalid had an idea. He found a phone in the corner of the room and punched in the number of his best friend Mounir. *Listen,* he told Mounir, *I want to introduce you to my new friend, Irene. Can you meet us in a few minutes at The Escape for a drink?* Mounir immediately agreed.

Mein Irene? Mounir asked in Arabic. *You'll find out,* Khalid said, also in Arabic. *I've fallen in love...*

When Irene came back downstairs, Khalid was rubbing his palms together, all smiles. *I've just arranged for you to meet my good friend, Mounir. So we're going to meet him for a drink nearby. How does that sound?*

While she was up in the bathroom she had been frantically wondering what to do next. Should she let him stay? Should she just see him to the door? Should she ignore the obvious facts and throw herself into this love? By the time she came back to the kitchen, she still didn't have any idea of what to do. And so she heard his plan with an inner smile. He had solved it himself. They would go for a drink together. That was all. She was eager to stretch out her time with this magical man, just a little bit more, just a little bit more, before the inevitable goodbye. *Why not*, she said to him, *that sounds good.*

The minute they stepped off of her front porch together, he grabbed her hand and held it tightly as they walked to the bar. And she knew that she was walking, hand to hand, finger to finger, heart to heart with a man who would soon bring her pleasure.

The pain part had already begun.

5
Some Little Known Facts
About the Whole Thing

A feeling is a dull thought.
A thought is sharper than a wing in the night.

She wasn't traveling at all. Ever.
And there was no original love.

There was a home, but it had something
To do with liquid.

Memory recirculated
But not through voice box.

She was once a child alone in her room, daydreaming about what it would take to communicate the simple idea of love to the world. The idea that compassion was the thing that binds people together. She was gazing out the window of her room at a dogwood tree in full bloom. Its white blossoms were springing to life in the morning sunlight. In her life, she had never experienced the cutting of a single tree.

At breakfast, she told her parents that she'd like to throw a giant love party where everyone would come, and no one would talk about anything except good and beautiful and meaningful things.

You're getting worked up again, her mother told her, *calm down and eat.* Breakfast was French toast and fresh strawberries and orange juice; it was her first lesson that the fruits of the earth mean nothing when the heart is alone.

Some of the facts about the whole thing

When you live among dead people, your own skin begins to turn cold.

They may be dead, but they still read *Time* magazine and *Newsweek* and are always more informed about the world than you. And you'll never persuade them that, since they are dead, their perception might be a little skewed. You can't convince them that there *was* no chemical weapons factory in Sudan. That those are actual people in Iraq, in trenches, hospitals, on the highway of death.

But the worst part of living among the dead is that you yourself become reduced, by degrees, to their plane of existence. The coldness begins to penetrate. You learn deeply the routine of deadness. And you start to lose touch. First with your values, then your language, then your ability to feel or think at all. And when you become completely passive, you will go along with anything.

It happened to Irene. She called it her dead period. And when she finally realized it, she too became a fugitive from The Law. She became obsessed with things like keeping warm and finding the remainder of her species.

Some little known facts

In 1987 the world was close to ripeness, close to falling from its tree. And New Year's Resolutions were coming in from the coast in sets of seven.

There was a forgetful President in office—which left the whole world in a state of amnesia.

The year came with a yellowish tint like a frantic ambulance rounding the corner.

Or like a tranquilizer gun in the hand of a man with "the very best of intentions."

Only those who knew what to expect saw anything coming.

About the whole thing

Khalid was always a replacement for the original absence of love.

Khalid was never a replacement for the *idea* of love because he was so bloody real.

He was known by friends and enemies alike for his generosity, poetic sensibility, and his sharp sense of humor.

He was also known for his uncanny ability to fire out verbal retribution in precise proportion to the abuse that he himself had ever received.

When Irene finally noticed and mentioned this unhappy trait, he said, *this is what I call "maturity."* She told him it would be MUCH more mature if he took out his anger on those who truly deserved it. *That's not maturity*, he said with a smile, *that's revolution.*

These are the kinds of exchanges that took place soon after they had moved in together, two weeks after they met at the demonstration.

These friendly debates were held in the recess between heated bouts of sex. It was the kind of sex that always started in one room and somehow wound up in another. Neither of them directed their erotic migrations. Their bodies would just inch along the walls and floor involuntarily. The way two kittens wrestle—there was a lot of purring and pawing going on.

Then afterwards Khalid always made refreshments,

strawberries and orange slices arranged artistically on a plate, or olives and cheese with Arabic flat bread, and they'd lounge around, arguing some more.

He'd make ludicrous and annoying assertions:

> *If Stalin had only lived ten years longer, there would probably be world peace by now.*

> *The reason that poor Americans are so fat is their subconscious desire to assert superiority over starving people in Third World countries.*

> *If God had meant women to have orgasms, he would have given them penises. What's this clitoris thing? Such an inferior organ.*

Irene would become infuriated and start throwing things at him. She'd kick the wall, and storm out the door. She came to find out later that he never meant a word he said in those idle moments. Like the rhetoricians of ancient Greece, arguments were thrown out not for their truth-value, but for their overall effect. Above all he wanted to break the monotony, create a mood. He was attempting the impossible: to wake the dead.

Her only proof of his disloyalty to his own statements was his obvious loyalty to her so-called "inferior organ." He went to great lengths to see how much pleasure he could bring her. This was just one of the many reasons Irene never failed to return to their little attic apartment.

He would greet her at the door, sometimes only dressed from the waist down, with a mop of black curls falling across his eyes; and then he'd pour himself all over her and the whole thing would begin again. The epic journeys across floors, walls, rooms. Eventually they'd wind up in the shower.

Soaking, sometimes still half-dressed, they might as well have been insane.

Two shadow lovers moving slowly against a world of white.

I love you, they whispered together, looking without fear into the other's eyes, smiling. *I love you like crazy, crazy, crazy.*

More facts

From the day they had met they had become inseparable. They lived in each other's shadow. Every waking and sleeping breath was inhaled and exhaled from each other's air. No hour was too late for him to wake up clutching her, saying, *what rusty desert is this exile?*

No hour was too early for her to wake him in tears saying that she had been trapped inside a burning car, pounding on the windows, screaming for help.

They had too much time on their hands. As students, they were used to being poor and had no inclination to do anything about it.

Irene was twenty-two. Khalid was either twenty-four or twenty-six, depending on whether you counted the years he called 'the bad years.' The ones he didn't even include as part of his life.

More facts

If you put your ear to the train track, listening, the way they do in old Westerns, it doesn't make the train come faster.

And if you put a bunch of trumped-up, secondary facts out on the table, it doesn't make the real facts go away:

The pain was sharp, cyclical, and deadly. It would disappear for a time on its circuit, like a wide round blade, moving to a point that was distant and invisible. And then it would make its way back, cutting sharper and deeper. The knowledge was unavoidable, cyclical, and deadly—Irene had fallen in love with someone who was already taken.

There was a history there; and even if Khalid insisted that it was an inferior history, built on youth and desperation, it was still a history, which Irene had interrupted.

Khalid told her again and again that it wasn't a real marriage. It was just for the papers. He and Bernie had only gotten married so that he could get away from a war zone. It wasn't even his idea—Sarah had arranged it all. He had told Bernie from the beginning that there would be no long-term commitments. *I have always been honest. I don't like to play games. As soon as I fell in love with you, I told her immediately.*

This was all assuaging; the blade would retreat.

Weeks went by

Soon it was summer and they'd lie around in their underwear and t-shirts listening to music, trying to move as little as possible. Irene turned him on to American classics like Bob Dylan, Charlie Parker, Billie Holiday. He introduced her to Arab icons: Fairouz, Farid al-Atrache, and Umm-Kalthoum. While they were lying there letting the last chords of music sift through them, he would teach her all the love and sex words in Arabic. *Love words and sex words in Arabic,* he'd insist, *are one and the same. We're such a romantic culture we haven't separated the two.* He'd hold her and say, *When I whisper, "Ya Hiati" into your ear, it means that I am ready to merge with you—body and soul.*

Then, just to show her how it worked, he'd whisper *I love you* tenderly again and again and again deep into her ear; and his theory turned out to be correct. Soon she'd be melting, melting from head to toe.

Days would go by, and she wouldn't think about their situation. Then the phone would ring.

The phone had a special ring to it when it was Bernie on the line. Irene could hear the anger fomenting between the first and the second ring. Against her better judgment, she once picked it up. It was Bernie in the middle of a breakdown. *How can you do this?* Bernie cried. *Don't you know what this is doing to me? I am crumbling. I'm falling apart. You shit. You both are shit.*

She went on like this for a few minutes. She said that she had sacrificed five years of her life and that Khalid had used her to get his citizenship and that he was nothing but a piece of crap. Finally she slowed down saying, *Don't you have anything to say?*

Irene held her breath. There was nothing to say. She thought about telling her, *Okay go ahead and take him.* But she knew she'd never do it, because she wasn't about to let him go.

And so there was nothing to say.

Just then Khalid walked in, stopping at the door. He had a disturbed look on his face—he had obviously just had a run-in with some public atrocity… a homeless person being detained by the cops. A biased anti-Arab news report on the radio. A pile of pesticide-covered, non-union grapes at the store.

It's Bernie, Irene mouthed to him silently.

Don't you have anything to say? Bernie asked again in the vacuum that had grown wider and more desperate. Irene felt caged between the two of them, Khalid's visible anger and Bernie's accusatory voice.

It's like the blind leading the blind, Irene finally answered. Then before she could add more to this statement, she slowly hung up the phone.

It's like the blind leading the blind? Khalid asked. *It's like the blind leading the blind? What's that supposed to mean?*

She wasn't sure if what he wanted was an English lesson, though she vaguely gathered that he knew what the phrase meant.

The blind leading the blind—it means we've taken a wrong turn, Irene said. *We're lost…*

Is that true? he said with a slightly bitter tone, *Are you lost? Are you blind? You didn't mention that fact when I met you.* He walked past her and went straight into the kitchen with his bag of groceries.

What happened to you? Irene asked over the counter that divided the kitchen from the rest of the room, *Why are you in such a bad mood?*

He was happy to tell her: *It's simple,* he said, unpacking the Ralph's bag on the counter. *I can't stand Capitalism. Look at these vegetables they are trying to sell us! This is not a tomato, it's plastic!* He held a scentless yellowish tomato right up to her nose. *Can you smell ANYTHING? A tomato should smell like a tomato, not like wax.*

He started putting the few things he had bought into the refrigerator continuing, *What did Bernie say? It's her fault that I wound up in this genetically-engineered society. Bernie doesn't really have a problem with the whole setup here. That's why no matter how much we tried, we could never get along.*

I can't believe that she's the one who's suffering, and you're mad at her, Irene said with indignation.

She's good at being a victim, he said as he started to cook dinner. *She should take responsibility for her own bad decisions.* Khalid wasn't a cupboard and door slammer when he was upset. That was Irene. When he was irritated, his actions took on a keen and deliberate precision. The slow and steady way he attended to things was an indication of ruffled angry thoughts. He must have had a flash of some memory of his life with Bernie—there was brooding in the way he lined up the vegetables from largest to smallest near the cutting board. And in the exact way he slit the plastic wrap of the meat package, in one perfect slash.

I'm making "hoasi," he said as if answering a question she'd never asked. *It's just a quick stew for when you can't think of anything else to cook.* He was trying to calm the air.

She was silent and went to lie down on the futon. She looked out the window where the sun was on its way down. For a few minutes she watched Khalid move around the kitchen. The delicate bone structure of his tanned angular face, his agile grace as he stirred the pot, wiped counters, swept the floor, were almost wounding. She kept hearing Bernie's voice over and over in her head, *I'm crumbling. I'm falling apart....* Bernie's despair was present in the room.

Why do I get the feeling that there's more to your marriage than you ever told me? It feels like there's a lot of unfinished stuff. Irene spoke from the place she was sitting.

You don't ever leave someone completely behind, Khalid said. *They always remain a part of you.* He stirred his stew in the quiet space his own words had opened. In the meantime, she leaned over and put a Dylan tape in the machine. Harmonica twanged and Dylan's voice jangled out, filling the room with a kind of conciliatory air.

Something there is about you that lights a match in me.
Is it the way your body moves or the way your hair
blows free?

But Irene didn't want to let the discussion go.

Why does Bernie say that you used her for the green card? she asked casually, trying not to sound like the Spanish Inquisition. Khalid placed the food on the back burner, turned off the kitchen light, and walked over. Standing above her he said, *We have an expression in Arabic: When the camel's down on the ground, everyone is ready to stick their knife into it.*

I can't believe YOU are using a camel metaphor! She reminded him of his own dislike of these "Orientalist" clichés.

That's not the point now, he replied, sitting on the floor a few feet away from her. *What I'm saying is that people are always ready to go on the attack, without justification, especially when they know I can't do anything about it.*

Number one, whatever Bernie did, she did willingly. Number two is that I never used her. Ever. If anything she used me.

The way he said this last thing was so cold that she left it without a response.

Dylan was still singing with his stone-tumbler voice about the end of love, the beginning of love, twilight on the frozen lake. Khalid came over and he lay on top of her lengthwise and then he placed his salty lips on hers and whispered, *I can't help it if I love you. I just do. When everything is said and done, you remain the lightest and the most profound. Thank God we have each other.*

He put his head on Irene's chest for a minute; and the music and the world and the round sharp blade cut through them.

More of the facts

It was about this time that Khalid finally met Kathy, who had just come back from New York. Khalid and Kathy understood each other immediately as soon as Irene introduced them; they were cut from exactly the same confrontational cloth. Things that he might not like in anyone else—endless graphic obscenity, dykish tendencies, obsession with the physical body—he respected in Kathy, because she was so smart.

Whenever Khalid made one of his wild unsubstantiated assertions, Kathy always understood it on the very level that it was offered. She understood hyperbole; it was her own strong suit. She understood the need to *wake the dead.*

And whenever Kathy made one of her elliptical statements that could either mean everything or nothing at all, Khalid would roll and dive with it.

The only reaction against an unbearable society is to write equally unbearable nonsense, she said as an explanation of her sociopathic, illegible novels.

I know, I know. Power, language. We Palestinians know the meaning of cultural dismemberment.

But you can't get to a place, to a society, that isn't

constructed according to the phallus. I guess you Arabs know about that too?

Okay, but our male-dominated society is still less phallic than America, believe me. Believe me.

Right, think of Jean Genet's "Prisoner of Love."

Genet? Actually, I love Genet. He's an exception.

Exception to what?

Most of your other hip French theorists wouldn't survive one day in an Israeli or an Arab prison. One minute of torture and they'd be turning their mothers in....

People only think and act as their objective conditions allow.

Objective conditions. Now, that's a phrase I hate. I hate that phrase as much as I hate...as much as I hate U.S. foreign policy....

Irene would participate in these discussions, but there was something about the energy that sprang up between Khalid and Kathy that was hard to come between. Like jazz improvisationists, everything was call and response between them.

When a conversation was particularly intense it was Irene who would volunteer to go out to the Vietnamese shop down the street for some takeout noodle soup and spring rolls. She would do so happily, willing to do anything to keep her two friends together in her presence.

Irene never felt that Khalid was being monopolized by Kathy. On the contrary, she was pleased that they got along, since her other friends didn't like him. They didn't even try to hide their knee-jerk distrust of him.

Her ex-roommate J.D. had told her at one of their house-meetings before she moved out: *We're concerned about you, Irene. We don't know anything about this guy. We have no idea what he's involved in.*

Like what? Irene asked. *What are you worried about in particular?*

You know, Arabs, their patriarchal culture for example.

The liberals in her circle had their causes; they were involved in border issues, Latin America, the Black struggle, and feminism, but none of them knew much about Palestine or the Arab world. *If there is to be a World War III*, they might say, *it will be started by some psychopathic Arab dictator.*

When Irene reminded them that it was the United States who was stockpiling nuclear weapons like there was no tomorrow and who had actually *used* them, they went against their own liberal politics to argue that "we" had learned our lesson about them.

You guys are so racist it makes me sick, Irene slammed down her cup. *You'd never say that kind of stuff if I were in love with a Black man or a Mexican.* She decided at that point to move out of the house.

Kathy didn't have these reactions to Khalid at all. Kathy was, as she said—"post-identity." Her entire life work was about breaking down false dichotomies, the social structures, the politics that keep people alienated from their natural ties to each other.

But Kathy was leaving again for New York, where she was spending more and more time. And soon enough it was Irene and Khalid again, alone in a world that seemed to be against them.

More of the facts

It was after that disagreement with her roommates that Irene had moved in with Khalid. They rented the cheapest place they could find in the ugliest part of town. Aesthetics were thrown out the window; the attic apartment had no charm, no chic. It was located next to a boulevard that was an endless series of auto repair shops, fast food restaurants, tire outlets, and any other kind of business that lacked even a shred of beauty.

The luxurious California of the coast had nothing in common with these neighborhoods further east. Every bungalow had an apartment building looming behind it. Every apartment building had a garage that had been converted to a cheap living space.

The area was populated by refugees from wars around the globe. Ethiopians and Eritreans lived side-by-side in this new land. A few blocks down it was the South Vietnamese. Then further out, sprinkled a little bit everywhere, there were the Central Americans. These neighborhoods were a run-down stretch of crime and broken homes. Trash floated through the empty lots and alleys, picked up only by the wind.

By midsummer, the world seemed sluggish and unfair. To change their mood, Khalid and Irene sometimes drove west and took sunset walks in the city park. It was during these strolls that they managed to relax a little. Sometimes they'd lie in the grass and kiss and whisper to each other far into the night.

In my language, he'd say, *the land is a woman, and woman is the land. Do you see? We haven't just lost a homeland. We've lost our mother. Our sister. Our lover...*

Why did I have to meet you like this? Irene said. *Why couldn't we have started completely clean? Without hurting anyone. Without so much pain?*

Hake.

Hake? she asked. *What's hake?*

That's just the way it is. It also means "like this."

Like this?

Yes, he said in a low voice, *now kiss me, because I refuse to stop loving you. Touch me.* Irene held him and caressed him.

Like this? Hake? she asked.

Hake.

More facts

One evening Irene and Khalid were on one of these sunset walks in the park. They were strolling along, smelling flowers, watching the nervous flight of a little hummingbird. They found some amazing seed pods on an odd tree they had never seen before. The pods were soft-skinned and curved in an inward spiral to a center that held a core of sticky seeds. They examined the pods with fascination. They became children again, mesmerized. Khalid especially had a deep love for discovering the seductive secrets of nature.

After examining the seeds and discussing these beguiling constructs of the natural world, they somehow became involved in a discussion about evolution and history. Irene concocted a theory that everything in the world was really about color, attraction, and desire. She hypothesized that human destiny was probably less about survival and more about desire. *Desire*, she told him, *is really the essential force compelling all human change, all progress in human history.*

Khalid gave this some thought, then disagreed. *No,* Khalid shook his head emphatically, *It's still Will to Power. That's the essential force. Will to Power.*

Okay, she answered, *but if humans weren't filled with desire, nothing else would happen at all.*

Why do you always see everything as sexual? he asked abruptly.

The tone changed from a casual discussion to something sharper with a cutting edge. Irene tensed up, preparing for a conflict.

I'm not even talking about sexual desire, Khalid. I'm talking about the impulse for growth, for transcendence, for progress.

Progress? he scoffed. It was a habit of his to stop walking whenever he wanted to make a point. They stood for a minute under a towering eucalyptus tree while he grasped her arm almost frantically, saying, *What progress are you talking about? Brute force has always been and still is the name of the game.*

After he spoke, Irene was the one to start walking again. She started gesticulating wildly, *Life! It's all about Desire!*

People wanted things. Wanted to do things. "Urge, urge, *always the procreant urge*," she quoted Walt Whitman.

Khalid stopped dead in his tracks again. *The history of humanity,* he said, pausing between each of his words with a keen and deliberate precision, *is a history of blood, conquest, and coercion. No one changes without being FORCED to change.*

In less than five minutes a simple conversation had turned into a dispute that brought them close to physical violence. There it was in a nutshell: their two opposing worldviews were laid bare. Irene trembled with rage at his unwillingness to give even the slightest consideration to her point of view. He was boiling too. And worse yet, he was profoundly disappointed that she seemed so myopic, so petit-bourgeois, so utterly enchanted with the world, that she couldn't see the horrible suffering wrought by humans, with human hands.

They were walking along, stopping and starting, arms waving, voices transformed into sharp-edged weapons. Irene threw down the little pods she was carrying and said, *I'm leaving. I can't stand your arrogance....* He grabbed her arm again saying, *Don't do your typical cowardly run away from a fight thing.* Irene stayed, but not without responding: *It's not considered cowardly to put as much distance as possible between myself and an abominable....* She couldn't think of a good noun to follow "abominable" other than "snowman" so she just left the sentence hanging. They continued walking side by side in morose silence, each of them inwardly trying to think of the one brilliant argument that would finally bring the other person to his or her senses.

As they walked, Irene saw someone sitting slumped on a park bench in front of them. When they got closer, it turned out to be Khalid's best friend, Mounir. He was a Palestinian too, born in the Shatila refugee camp in Beirut. He had left on a scholarship several years before the Israeli invasion. His mother and sister never got out, and didn't survive the three-day massacre in the camps.

Mounir was sitting by himself on a bench, smoking a cigarette, looking up at the sky.

Khalid came up to him, and without so much as a hello or a greeting, asked him straight away: *We need you to solve a dispute here, Mounir. Is it* Desire *or* Will to Power *that has had more influence on human history?*

Mounir's face brightened immediately when he looked up and saw his friends. But then his smile changed again when he saw that they were obviously enmeshed in a fight. He put out his cigarette with his shoe and said, *What are you two doing, arguing about such stupid stuff? For God's sake.*

No, Mounir, Khalid continued, *Solve it for us once and for all. Desire or Will to Power?*

Mounir looked down at the ground and slowly repeated the words to himself, *Desire or Will to Power....Finally* he looked up and spoke. *It's both.*

Khalid smiled saying, *You're so diplomatic.*

No, I just thought of an example. For thousands of years, humans dreamed of flying. They longed to fly. And they finally did it. They finally devised a way to get off the ground...

See? Irene interrupted triumphantly. *Mounir understands* exactly *what I'm trying to say.*

But then Mounir turned to her and with great disgust said, *And just think how fast they started using those wonderful planes to bomb people, just think.*

There was silence. No one said anything. Mounir turned away, looking up at the sky again, squinting, even though the sun was already setting. He reached into his breast pocket for another cigarette. Khalid and Irene looked at each other, waiting to see what would happen next. Finally Mounir spoke. *But it isn't worth fighting about, for God's sake.* In a muffled voice he said, *Let's go get drunk.* He was still looking off at the sky. Suddenly he turned and looked at his friends, *Come on, let's go.*

Yallah N'iskar, Ya Mounir, Khalid said with exaggerated cheerfulness. *Let's go get drunk.* He held out his hand to help Mounir up from the park bench. *Ya Halla, Habibi* he said and they hugged and kissed. It was their first real greeting. *Ahlain, Ahlain,* Mounir kept saying over and over again. Then they walked together, arm in arm the three of them, up to their favorite hangout, The Escape.

A little-known fact

There are two lives in every life.
The one that you live.

And the one you remember.

History is what falls. In between. History is what you write down—sometimes to remember, sometimes to forget.

Sometimes to avoid the harshness of the facts, and sometimes to make sure that your own version of the facts is not erased forever.

Khalid's version of the facts

He was a loyal person. He had never hurt another soul in his life.

He felt torn because deep down he knew that he was guilty of betraying Bernie, a person who had helped him in hard times. Even though their marriage was, as he had always said, "not a real marriage," he knew too that she had loved him. He knew that he owed her something, and that the pain she was enduring wasn't fair.

The idea that he had actually wounded a friend was a horror to him. He also happened to be missing some books and notes that he needed for a newspaper article he was writing.

He only went back to Bernie's apartment to retrieve the

books he had left there. It had no symbolic weight, he said. It was simple. He thought she'd be at work. He honestly didn't know she had changed her teaching schedule. But she was there at home when he arrived.

Bernie thought that he was returning to her when he showed up at the door. She was crying and he felt he should console her the only way he knew how. It was the first time she had even seen him since he moved in with Irene. They spent many hours talking, fighting, talking, fighting. Then she asked him to spend the night, and he agreed.

It's so complicated, he told Irene the next day, *It was just my way of saying a final goodbye. I hope you can understand that.*

Irene's version

Khalid didn't show up all that evening. She waited and waited. She listened to one of his Fairouz tapes, missing him. She made herself coffee and read Frantz Fanon for an hour before falling asleep on the futon. She slept poorly, waking up every few hours to see if he had come home. When she woke up in the morning, still no Khalid. She called his two best friends, Mounir and Aziz, an Algerian. But they hadn't seen him. She went out to get the newspaper and when she came back he still wasn't home.

It was hours later when she was scouring the employment section of the newspaper that he finally walked in, looking exhausted.

What happened to you? she asked.

He didn't want to tell her. Instead he said, *What are you doing with the newspaper? Are you looking for a job? Good idea, we need some money around here.*

What happened to you? Irene asked again. He went to the fridge and searched for something to drink. Coming up with nothing, he poured himself a glass of tap water. *Come here,* he said.

No, you come here.

She felt as though a small fist-sized organ—her heart— had dropped down into her stomach from above. There was something heavy in the pit of her gut that didn't belong there.

He walked over and said, *the truth is, I was with Bernie last night.* As soon as he said it, she knew exactly what had happened. It was written all over his face.

It's finally over, he continued, *I've been through something major tonight, and I can't talk much now.*

Irene felt as though she was being shredded inside. The blade that had been revolving in a wide circular path was now whirring back and forth, as if stuck in a position called "slash wide open."

I'm so fuckin' sorry, Khalid kept saying, *I'm so fuckin' sorry.* Then he disappeared into the bathroom for a long time, and Irene could hear the muted sounds of his weeping, and she knew that he was.

Some little known facts

When you have lived for many years among the dead, you find later that you possess all the secret mechanisms of deadness.

Dead people are those who have been lying to themselves for so long, they have forgotten the truth. They live their lies, recreate lies, give birth to new lies. They surround themselves only with those people who are willing to participate in their fictions.

These people may be dead but they are your friends and your family who still love and care about you. They feel that the best way to teach you to survive in a brutal world of possible tragedy and impossible emotions is to lead you at all times toward the path of least resistance.

And you start to lose touch. With your values, your language, your ability to feel or think at all. And then when you become completely passive, you make an astonishing discovery—there is a natural appeal to an inert form of existence.

Irene began, after his night out, to go back to this way of life. Instead of confronting the situation head on, she simply turned off.

How easy it was. To become an emotional wall. To ignore the vicious blade that had refused to budge from its whirring position. It was an instinct buried deep within her—to pretend that the hurtful thing had never happened. To move forward blindly without taking stock.

She set her inner thermometer at slightly above freezing, and waited to see what would happen.

It so happened

that the issue of making money now became a convenient necessity. Both Khalid and Irene put their personal conflicts on the back burner and threw themselves into that task. Job-hunting became a pastime, a hobby, a passion.

Khalid, for his part, would write out long "pros and cons" lists for every possible occupation. He would come home from the library with pamphlets, career questionnaires, and job-search manuals. He took them all very seriously. *If you are going to get a job, you have to have a system*, he'd say. *You have to find out as much as possible about your range of options.* He spent an entire afternoon filling out a career profile quiz. In the end it said that with his skills and disposition he was best suited for a career in investment banking.

It was a sudden revelation, a whole world he had never contemplated. *There's a lot of upward mobility in banking. I'll work my way to the top; I'll bide my time,* he said rubbing his palms together, *and once I get there, I'll make thousands of low-interest loans to poor people who never get access to money!*

Though he went on several interviews, he did not get hired at a bank. He did, however, get a job at 7-11. He was enthusiastic about that, too. He went to work the first day in a pressed white shirt and tie. The second day Khalid was up early again, ironing his clothes.

By the third day, he realized what a bad deal the whole thing was—the smell of hotdogs and nachos, the sticky spills beneath the soda dispenser, the late night drunks wandering around for hours near the candy displays. By the fourth day, Khalid was talking to the other 7-11 workers about the need to form a labor union. On the fifth day he was fired.

When Kathy asked Khalid why he was fired, he said: *They told me I was "lacking in judgment."*

Oh, replied Kathy, *the old "lacks judgment" excuse. That's what boring people in power use against people who are spiritually superior. Congratulations!*

While Khalid continued on his quest for the perfect job, a quest that would end up lasting for years, Irene started waiting tables at a little Italian bistro. Although she had once vowed, *Never again!* she donned the old apron and began serving pasta with a half-baked smile. She worked almost every evening, bringing home cash that would be gone by the next afternoon.

About the cash thing

With Irene out working, Khalid was doing the shopping and cooking. He bought all the delicacies and special drinks that they had been missing. He cooked elaborate Palestinian meals during the day—enough to feed scores of guests. And by the evening, he was entertaining the masses. People Irene had never even seen before showed up eagerly to enjoy Khalid's hospitality. Old friends of his and Bernie's started reappearing in his life in droves. She was amazed by the number of people he knew.

Irene actually started to wonder if there was another expression in Arabic about how when the camel is back up on its feet—everyone wants to go for a ride.

Ever since the night that Khalid spent with Bernie, however, Irene began to view things differently. It was impossible for her to truly enjoy those evenings of food and entertainment. Although their attic became filled with jokes, storytelling, laughter, and even tears, Irene felt outside of it all. She would often grouch around in the corners, resentful of having their privacy interrupted.

Sometimes at midnight, Mounir unpacked his violin and Aziz brought out his *oud* and they all started singing folk tunes. First a lone voice would call out a sad plaintive tune, and then after an interval, the rest of the people would enter into the song, clapping and drumming and chanting the same refrain. The music would alternate between that single voice offering some kind of poetic complaint against the world and the whole group—raising a loud clamor in the night.

For the first time in her life Irene developed a conscience about "bothering the neighbors."

It was also during this period that Irene began to notice that some of the poetry that Khalid had whispered to her earlier in the spring was being recycled for new occasions. This was particularly annoying to her. There was a line that he had recited to her back when they fell in love. *I'm anxious as if the wind were beneath me.* Irene had always assumed that it was *his* invention, inspired by *her*, his muse. Now she discovered by accident that it was a line from a famous ancient poet, al Mutannebi.

You schmuck! She rebuked him when she found out. *I thought you wrote that line!*

In the beginning Irene used to ask Khalid to translate the anecdotes and jokes to her, but more and more she would creep off on her own and read a book or write in her journal. Or go to sleep early, complaining bitterly that he and his friends ought to keep the noise down.

Or more and more she would just stay away. She started going out for drinks with the other waitresses and restaurant employees after work. She began to contemplate other love arrangements. She imagined that she had been mistaken all along, that this love was not unique after all.

A tour of the ruins
The color of everything is the color of mourning

A tour of the house of al-Andalus
The forgotten path to the gardens

In the dream of defeat
delicate creations are thrown to the sea.

Was it me who left last night
or did you leave me?

Or was it the stranger within each of us
Slowly taking leave, step by step, before the final farewell?

One night in the last weeks of summer, Irene came home very late, at two in the morning. Scattered about were all the telltale signs that Khalid's friends had been there—empty bottles, dirty plates on the counter, ashtrays overflowing with cigarette stubs and ashes. But the people were all gone now, and the place was dark and empty. And so was Irene. She was hoping that Khalid would be asleep, for on this particular night she had much to hide.

But when she looked to the corner, Khalid was lying with his arms folded behind his head, eyes open. He was lying in wait. He saw that she saw him, but neither of them even said hello. A full moon was shining through the blinds, casting his face and upper body in uncanny stripes. He looked more like a something than a someone. Irene now felt the distance between them. She realized that she didn't know him at all. She didn't know his language, his thoughts and dreams, the tragedies of his past.

Irene walked over slowly and began to undress, saying nothing. She lay down beside him. They lay like frozen statues for several minutes. She felt his coldness toward her growing by the minute.

Then his voice broke the silence. *Oh stranger of the house*, he began, his face still covered with glowing stripes. *Oh stranger of the house...*

Is that your poem, Irene interrupted in an acid tone, *or someone else's?*

*Love is all secrets...*he kept going, reciting more lines nonstop. She was filled with dread. She felt the truth of these haunting words run through her veins.

Stop it, Irene told him, *I'm not in the mood for poetry.*

He stopped reciting and said in a dead slow voice, *I called your friends looking for you. They said they hadn't seen you.*

So? she said, waiting for more.

I called the restaurant. Your boss told me you left early. So?

Then where were you? You were out on a date, weren't you? He paused then added, *Don't tell me no. I can feel it. I'm clairvoyant about these things.*

She thought about lying but then became brave. *Yes,* she told him, *you're clairvoyant.*

Who is he? Khalid asked, still lying on his back, looking straight up at the ceiling.

No one. Just someone I met at the restaurant.

Khalid fell silent and then all of the sudden he turned his back to her.

Turn around, Irene said to him. But he stayed with his back to her, giving her the silent treatment. *Turn around,* she begged. But he didn't move.

Well, why shouldn't I? she cried pulling hard on his shoulder.

Why shouldn't I? she shrieked, and began to get hysterical. *You were the first to betray me.* Irene pounded on his back. *You slept with her! You asshole. You fucker. You're the one who screwed up every good thing between us. Now everything is broken.*

She began weeping violently on Khalid's neck. Finally he turned around abruptly asking her, *Did you sleep with him?*

No, she sniffled. Then she added in a clearer voice, *but I wanted to.*

Then why didn't you? Khalid sat upright with his back to the window. Now the stripes were gone and in their place a long shadow covered the whole of his face.

You know why, she said.

No, I don't know why, he said loudly, bitterly. *If everything is BROKEN between us, why not just do whatever you want.*

You know why! she screamed back.

No, I don't. If everything is so broken, why did you even bother coming home?

Irene did not know what to say at moments like these, moments where everything was collapsing inward upon her. Words abandoned her, like frightened sailors jumping ship in a panic. Later, she would wake at dawn and scribble a note, a letter, a poem, some string of words that might, like a net, collect everything—the fears, accusations, apologies, feeling of bereftness. But not in the middle of the action, never. Now she was mute, frozen, had nothing to say.

You know why, she said again, stalling for time until she could think of some way to turn the whole thing around once and for all. But she never did.

And so the empty, hurtful conversation went on and on like that all night. And into the next day. And into the coming years. And this was to become the simmering unsettled dispute, fracturing whatever good times were to be had. *Was it me who left, or did you leave me?* Each of them was always inwardly trying to think of the brilliant argument that would establish, once and for all, who had destroyed their innocence.

But Irene always kept one secret that she dared not admit to Khalid.

On that very night when she came back from her date, and when they had that fight, Irene privately came to an understanding. She now understood that Khalid had won the argument—the one about Desire and Will to Power. She never could have conceded this loss because it would have meant a more horrifying defeat than can be admitted to a lover.

Because after her date that night, after she had very nearly slept with another man, after she had come close to throwing her fate in with a random stranger, she came back to Khalid. She came back, compelled not by desire. Desire, raw desire, was what she had for the man she had just met. But she came back to Khalid under the sway of something more compelling than desire.

And that was power.

6
"Lissa Fakir"

If Irene were to tell the story, she would tell it in spurts, in starts, in fragmented notes. It would be like some ill-made, reject, jigsaw puzzle, where none of the pieces were even designed to fit. Readers would ask themselves, *What the hell is this?*

Irene was not a storyteller at heart. She didn't trust her own memory or imagination.

She felt transparent.

Like raindrops hanging from a storefront awning in springtime. Or as if a pack of arrows had gone through her in one shot—she felt that her body and spirit had been turned into Swiss cheese.

In the months that passed since that first big falling out, it was Irene who was always on the defensive. Of the two, it was she who was considered wrong; it was she who had "stepped outside of the arrangement;" it was she who seemed to be seeking an escape. Though their bodies and routines grew more familiar, their minds' ability to meet in the lands beyond the "she" and the "he" was stifled at all times.

They often sat side-by-side as guests, waiting for whatever it would be—a beer, coffee, or in one case watery noodles. Irene was always mesh-like—inviting him to be part of her, or caught up in her.

The person they were waiting for was always in the next

building over. She'd see the shadow or silhouette in a towering window. Like the specter of an ex-lover, that's how it felt—the oppressive weight of the past.

Waiting on the couch, Khalid would suddenly reach over and grab her knee. She'd feel the hand go through the skin and straight up to her heart.

Had he learned to see through her?

He *had* learned to see through her.

He'd say: *You know what? You're crazy.* And she'd say, *It's YOU who made me crazy.* But she knew that he had known her.

He'd call her a slut and a whore. And she knew that he had managed to read all of her secret pornographic thoughts.

I should take you to the refugee camp in Beirut where I lived, so you can see what real suffering is.

She felt transparent.

From the beginning she convinced herself that he was the smarter of the two. He had honed his spirit and senses on some rough moments and she liked this for a change— someone who hadn't been pampered and reduced to a series of vapid reactions.

And the thing was, she was addicted to him from the very start, to the salty smell of him between chin and neck, scrotum and leg. After a year together she told him, *I'll never be the one to leave you. If this is going to end, you'll have to be the one to do it.*

What she didn't know about yet, even after all this time together, was her own power.

He would drive around the block no less than four times looking for the entrance to the eastbound freeway. He backed up, blocked traffic, went the wrong way down a one-way street. She said, *Look, Khalid. The sun is rising in THAT direction. Go. That's east.*

Finally they'd be heading straight into the morning sunlight. The dazzling rays would reach all the way through her, burning a sting into her eyes. Had they really stayed awake all night? Had they fought all night under streetlights near the ocean? Had he really said all those things?

How could you have had any feelings for that phony professor, Jules? I can tell you're still obsessed with him. Everything you said at their house was directed straight to him. Agh! I can't believe you almost slept with him!

It was a mistake! And besides, it was before I even met you! I never should tell you anything. You always find a way to use it against me.

Even if you didn't tell me, I would have known. By the way, your taste in men makes me sick.

Almost every discussion between them could lead to a confrontation. Even a simple one about what to do on a Friday evening. If she said, *Let's go see someone?* he'd say, *I can't stand anyone right now.* If she said, *Let's go out for a drink?* he'd say, *what for?* If she asked, *Why do you have to be so difficult?* He'd say:

I take life seriously. I'm not always in the mood for distractions.

There was a Snickers bar on the dashboard. The night before, when they were driving home from Sarah and Jules' house, it kept sliding back and forth every time he turned the car. Snickers bar to the left. Snickers bar to the right. The whole time he was berating her, she kept watching it. In the shadows where he parked the car, the brown oblong bar looked almost obscene, like a piece of crap. She kept looking at it, even when she started crying,

I know you're right about some things...

You should just see yourself. Flirting all night with that pretentious sucker. You selfish motherfucker! he said, slamming the steering wheel.

She looked around the car, outraged. The candy bar caught her eye again. The perfect weapon. She picked the thing up and threw it straight at his head. It hit him squarely on the nose. His face wore a shocked *how dare you* expression that said, *Impossible, impossible.* When she saw his dropped jaw, and his mouth hanging open, she started laughing. Just a teary sniffle at first. Then a giggle. When she saw a hint that his face had softened, she began to laugh out loud. He joined her.

Don't Snicker at me! he said. They laughed together.

Then he leaned over, saying *I'm sorry. I'm so sorry. You are perfect the way you are.... Thank God I met you.*

She'd say, *I don't know why I keep hurting you. I'm just an American brat.* They'd kiss. His mouth always had a sweet taste after a fight. As if in one toxic breath he had exhaled all of his bitterness. He'd put his lips on her neck saying, *God, I miss you. I love you like crazy.* And dive into her body as if it were water, as if he was so thirsty for even a single drop of tenderness.

Driving east in the morning toward the little cottage they had moved into together, she slumped down in her seat, exhausted. Her brain felt as though it had endured electro-shock therapy. They spent fifteen minutes looking for the highway. It felt like hours, and she sensed a revisitation of their terrible night. She tried to think of a word to say to pacify the air between them. Ripping open the candy bar she took a bite, trying to be nonchalant, and said:

I still can't get over how good your English is, for someone who's only been here a few years. That was a good pun, "How dare you snicker at me."

He looked at her and said, *I didn't say, "How dare you."*

Whatever. It was a good one.

That's what we Third Worlders do with all our free time, you know. We sit up under our kerosene lamps studying English, hoping one day for our big break.

She gave him a sideways look, to see whether he was sneering or smiling. He was smiling, with an unlit cigarette dangling from his lips. He rummaged around in the car door pocket next to him, then put on one of his favorite Egyptian cassettes. Umm Kalthoum. A classic: *Lissa Fakir.* The music erupted with a dramatic sweep of violins.

Lissa fakr, albi y'deeluk aman?
W'illah fakr, kilma hataeed il y kan?

Do you think my heart will allow me to trust you again?
Or that one word will bring back what used to be?

Come here, he would say at times like this, when the air
was too filled with outrageous unresolved tension.

And she'd move over, sitting on the middle bump, with a
seatbelt buckle jammed up against her ass. He'd drape his
arm around her, caressing her shoulder for a second or two.
Hunched down next to him, she'd look over at his right hand,
his tanned sensuous hand, resting on her shoulder, then
waving in the air to the passionate, rhythmical music. It was
a hand that was capable of anything.

7
Little Window

Many were the nights when Khalid's hand was an instrument of peace.

Many were the nights when Khalid's fingers became lightning rods drawing fire from Irene's body, conducting it to a place where it could do her no harm.

Some mornings, painful memories of an earlier life would flood back, and she'd remember episodes of humiliation and degradation that she hoped to forget. Khalid would find her curled up in a ball on the floor like a wounded animal, with no way to visualize a world beyond suffering. He would sit on the floor beside her.

Am I the cause of all these tears? he asked, as he drew his fingers across her forehead and down her back. She couldn't say yes, and she couldn't say no.

There was an old woman in my village who knew how to heal with her hands, Khalid told her quietly. *She used to place her fingertips on my forehead when I was sick. And she would whisper secretive prayers over me.*

Show me, Irene asked him. Khalid would place his fingers gently on her face and with downward strokes to her shoulders would erase all the misery from her. Sometimes he touched her "love spot," a special location on the center of her sternum. His barely audible whispers sounded like raindrops falling across the stained-glass windows of churches. She could feel the tension and sadness slipping away, replaced by peaceful images of colorful light.

It was as if Irene were stepping inside a mirror facing inwards. When looking in this direction, she found that her soul was exactly the shape that it was meant to be. She saw herself moving through watery passageways and then saw herself as part of these rivers, ever able to keep giving and flowing. There was a sound that went with these images. It was the sound of tiny pebbles splashing into sheltered water. As in a cave or a tunnel, the echo was as soft and reassuring as a heartbeat.

Painful memories dislodged from the frozen banks within her and floated off to places that were distant yet intimate. Like miniature ice floes, they were visible, but detached; she could see them in their entirety—receding into an interior distance, diminishing to the size of a pinprick.

When you touch me, she told Khalid, *I remember myself. What do you mean?*

I remember myself as a small child, she said. *I used to be overflowing with joy. I remember splashing through puddles in springtime. In my rain boots. The pink worms came up from the ground to soak in the wetness; yellow daffodils and crocuses were the first flowers to break out the dismal gray of winter. I was strong back then.*

You still have strength, Khalid said, *to be able to put up with your pain and mine too.*

Sometimes I wonder, Irene paused. *But it's your hands. Your hands bring me back.*

You can't have forgotten, Khalid said with a smile. *I've got the magic touch.*

You've got the touch, Irene replied, sitting up and stretching, then throwing her head down to his knee. *An angel of mercy.*

Maybe you can be the angel of coffee this morning, he cajoled her.

Ah, you schmuck, always after something!

But she pulled herself up from the floor and obliged his request, for it was always her wish to sustain whatever good feelings might arise between them. She could live without coffee, and without luxuries, and without many petty gratifications, but she could not live without hope.

Irene went straight to the kitchen, boiled a kettle of water, and placed two big spoons of coffee into the filter. When the water boiled, she poured it over the coffee grounds, listening to the patter of the liquid dripping into one of the cups. And all the while she grew wary as the distant ice floes slowly began to re-emerge within her and began their migration forward, looming large again.

Actually there weren't just a few soundless, lumbering icebergs on the distant horizon, there was an entire squawking menagerie of unresolved questions that could not be massaged away.

The heart of the matter was this: Irene's love affair with Khalid had become like riding a bucking bronco. Sharp hoofs and sharp words flying off at all angles were all but expected. Irene had a sense of accomplishment if she could remain balanced for more than fifteen seconds, but huddling on the ground had started to look like a good place to be.

She experienced Khalid as a dialectical figure in her life, bringing both beauty and regression. One step forward, two steps back. Or was it the other way around? It was impossible to say. He had brought her incalculable riches, and a wealth of dismay.

Khalid's mind was like a tightly wound fist, smashing its way through the universe. He was anything but ambivalent. Irene admired his certainty and passion, and had for a long time tried to emulate them. But it was pointless. She was never going to be like him, and she was now adjusting to that fact.

Irene saw herself as more flexible and fluid. She negotiated the strange passages within her with a combination of instinct and stubbornness. She believed in

subversion and compassion and didn't see things as either/
or. She was willing to compromise because she felt that was
the way people should act, and not just women. Meanwhile
it seemed that Khalid thought of these traits as weaknesses.

While the coffee was dripping, Irene sliced apples on a
plate, found some special cookies in the cupboard, and
arranged them on the tray. This morning ritual had taken on
the aura of a sacred act. She was contributing to an unspoken
pact that had evolved between them over time: *No matter
how far we descend into personal misery, we will always have
good food on hand.* Irene was beginning to believe that
attending to daily routines conscientiously was in itself an
act of resistance.

Resistance to what? Resistance to forces and voices that
seemed to want her to collapse, that wanted her to give up all
of her beliefs and goals. But that was impossible, wasn't it?
Even in her worst moments of turmoil, there was something,
some electric kernel of joy that rocked about inside her and
that seemed to generate language that came out in episodic
gushes.

In the past year Irene had finished her BA and had started
a graduate program in rhetoric and literature. She was an A
student, working on critical theory, feminism, and
postcolonial thought. She wrote brilliant, caustic papers and
presentations that made her an admired force in the
classroom; then she went home and wrote long poems of
erratic quality that she usually shoved into the hidden
recesses of the trashcan, covering them with orange peels
and ashes. She was certain that she would never write a
decent poem again; in fact she abandoned all hope of ever
becoming a poet.

Instead her preferred literary form had become the 20-
page, anxiety-ridden love letter, alternating between doubt,
anger, and passion. Quoting liberally from Rumi, Bob Dylan,
Saint Francis of Assisi, and Walter Benjamin, the letters were
the product of a convulsive, epileptic mind.

But it was a mind, nonetheless, bent on finding *le mot juste*.

She and Khalid had their good moments, of course. Several weeks earlier, during their spring break from classes, they went camping for a week in the Redwood Forest. There was something miraculous about the trip. At least at the beginning. They easily agreed on how to start a fire, where to pitch the tent, and what sort of foods to bring. They both agreed to transport only the basics: coffee, eggs, and any kind of protein that could be impaled on a stick.

In the daytime they walked amongst the towering redwood trees, marveling at each one, for each had its own personality and presence. Some of these fantastical, spirit-filled trees had survived forest fires hundreds of years earlier, and had huge gouged openings in their trunks. The two of them stood wide-eyed in these caves and pretended to be woodland sprites in a fairytale. Leaning against the inside of a tree, Khalid quoted a poem by Robert Louis Stevenson:

> *'Tis the season now to go*
> *About the country high and low,*
> *Among the lilacs hand in hand,*
> *And two by two in fairy land....*

Awestruck, Irene asked where, how, and why he had memorized a poem from *A Child's Garden of Verses*. He just smiled enigmatically and mumbled something about the British Empire's residue in his part of the world.

In the evening, they cleaned up their campsite together, reveling in the small pleasures of outdoor housekeeping. *Oh let's make this the trash area here!* they exclaimed, hanging a grocery bag from a tree. *Ah ha, here's a perfect place to put the coffee!* At night they skewered Polish sausages and roasted them over flickering orange embers.

Then under the light of the moon the sexual escapades began. In this arena, Irene still held her own, commanding

Khalid to perform creative sexual tasks one after the next. He willingly complied until they were both dripping wet, with enlarged glowing organs, and gasping for air in the sweaty little nylon enclosure.

The second night, Khalid improvised a puppet show with his phallus on the side of the tent with a flashlight. Irene had only seen people make dogs and ducks with the shadows of their hands. Irene laughed at the squeaking sound he used for the voice:

Help! I feel sick. I'm going to throw up, the puppet cried out in a tragically funny accent. Irene doubled over in laughter.

I'll help you! She dived over to nurse the suffering organ back to health.

No, you're making it worse! Get back! Khalid somehow made it shake its head back and forth, *No! No!* Irene attempted again to get in on the act.

Soon enough the shadows on the tent's rippling wall grew muffled and indistinct. The puppet became engulfed in the center of an undulating shadow, which was Irene.

I'm dyiiiinnng. Khalid's voice began to go out of character, becoming thick and slow.

Okay, shut off the flashlight, Irene pushed him over onto his back.

Now as Irene was pouring milk into their morning coffee in the cottage, she remembered that night in the redwoods and all of its pungent detail. She remembered how the universe had exhaled a breath of sex, pine resin, and the campfire smoke. After they had finished making love, they unzipped the tent flap so they could watch the moon migrating across the tips of the distant treetops, and they slept wrapped in each other's arms.

But Irene could not conjure that happy memory without also remembering the way that it had come to an end. Even as Irene put the milk back in the fridge, and prepared to bring the breakfast tray to Khalid, she recalled the trip's ill-fated conclusion

On the third morning, they were sitting by the fire drinking coffee, and they began to talk about Bernie. Bernie had recently married a union organizer from Long Beach, and, like a couple of retirees, the two of them moved to Phoenix together. Right before Bernie left town, she called Irene on the phone.

I have to thank you, Bernie said bluntly.

Why? asked Irene, *why in the world?*

Because if it weren't for you, I'd probably still be married to Khalid. Thank God you took him off my hands.

I wouldn't have left him on my own, Bernie admitted. *But it was the best thing that ever happened to me.*

Irene later told Khalid about Bernie's call. She told him about Bernie's moving plans, and some other minor details of the conversation. But she didn't bother to mention this part of the discussion, because Bernie's words had left her feeling irritated and confused. Now she decided to bring it up with Khalid.

They were sitting on two separate rocks by the smoldering fire. Wisps of smoke changed directions every few moments, blowing in her direction at first, then his. *By the way,* Irene blurted out, *did you know what Bernie said to me the other day?*

What's that? Khalid looked up.

She actually THANKED me for taking you away from her. She said she was grateful that I helped liberate her. From you.

Khalid listened to Irene recounting the discussion. He didn't have to ponder long to get the point. *I see,* he intoned, *now that she's got a new man, she's doing her best to poison us. You should have hung up on her.*

Irene thought about Khalid's immediate interpretation and response. She knew there were good reasons for his reaction. It HAD seemed that Bernie's comments were just short of vindictive. Bernie was essentially saying, *Getting rid of Khalid is the best thing that ever happened to me. And now you're stuck with him.*

But the conversation actually sent a wave of anxiety through Irene. She was not immune to the vertiginous, fearful feelings Bernie's words had provoked. *Khalid is an unhealthy addiction*, Bernie said. Did Bernie know something that she herself had yet to confront? Bernie's words reminded her of all her own bad feelings about Khalid.

Why should I have hung up the phone? Irene asked Khalid defensively, taking a sip of her cowboy coffee.

Because you shouldn't allow others to contaminate your thoughts...which you obviously have.

Khalid got up from the rock and started poking the fire with a long stick that began to glow at the tip. He waved the burning stick in the air in her direction and muttered something in Arabic that she didn't understand. No doubt it was some ancient proverb that warned all listeners to beware of the treachery of women. At least that was Irene's immediate interpretation.

What's that? Irene asked.

Nothing. Nothing to you.

They both looked down. Khalid continued poking at the fire and embers, until Irene finally blurted out what was really on her mind:

So Bernie's experience isn't relevant at all? She looked at him closely. She thought she now had him hooked on the ledge of some moral high ground, but he was already waiting in the bushes below.

Bernie's experience IS relevant to her, Khalid said, *but not to you and me.* He paused and looked her in the eye. *But we aren't talking about Bernie now, are we? We are talking about you.*

Irene started to say something then stopped.

I can read your insecurities, Irene.

Irene was quiet then, and so was he. Irene hadn't meant

to sound so confrontational. She didn't mean to spoil the mood by bringing up such a sensitive subject. Why did she have to talk about Bernie just then? She didn't know. She just wanted to get it off her chest. Now she inwardly choked on the knowledge of her mistake, but then again she wasn't going to back down or apologize, either.

Because there was the opposite impulse, too. *Why should there be taboo subjects?* she wondered to herself. Why is he so piercingly analytical about the fine distinctions of every encounter? Always on his guard, always poised for an enemy attack? She was tired of this posture.

And so they sat for a few minutes in silence, watching the last small log collapse to pieces, watching the fire turn to cinders, and the cinders to ashes. Khalid finally jumped up and threw his cup on the ground, saying, *I'm leaving. I'm leaving right now.*

She stood up too and they both packed up the camp without exchanging a single word. Khalid loaded the car with a great deal of overt glowering. Irene splashed water haphazardly into the fire circle, and picked up cigarette butts and trash, ironically remembering an old girl scout motto: always leave the campsite cleaner than you found it.

They got into the car and drove out of the forest, barely glancing at the majestic trees of the forest. They might as well have been in a forest of insignificant matchsticks. The only words spoken during the entire trip was when Khalid said, *Pull over, I need to go to the bathroom.*

As soon as they arrived home, they both peeled off their clothes and climbed into bed naked. They made up from the fight almost as soon as they hit the clean, cool sheets of home.

Irene now picked up the breakfast tray loaded with cookies and fruit and coffee and brought it to the bathroom where Khalid was taking a shower. Right when she arrived, he stepped out behind the curtain in all his naked glory. His long curls were dripping. His dark skin was glowing with an almost saintly shine. He dried himself vigorously with the air of someone who has only love—no hatred or shame—for his own physical presence. Everything about Khalid's tan, slim body signaled health, proportion, and beauty.

Khalid loves Irene, he wrote in the steamy mirror of the bathroom with the tip of his finger. Irene smiled. That was just a small sample of his inimitable charm. Just when it looked as if there was no juice left in the orange, he managed to squeeze one more drop, producing sweetness from thin air.

Only one day earlier when Irene asked him, *Do you still love me?* he replied, *Of course I love you. It's been well documented.* They laughed together at his funny way with words.

And here he was documenting it, yet again.

Khalid seemed to have an endless well of emotional resources to call upon even in his own dark hours. There was always the presence of some wise old woman in his words and actions.

But wasn't this his subconscious weapon, too? Irene wondered. He managed to prove, again and again, that he was the innocent one. That he was the lover, and she the betrayer. That he was simple in his desires, and she was too complicated. That if he lost his temper, it was because she had broken the trust between them; and that whenever he rose triumphantly to the occasion of forgiveness, it was evidence of his entire culture's richness and generosity.

Khalid never acted alone, but only in concert with a whole dispossessed people yearning to be free.

Irene balanced the tray on the sink. Khalid came up from behind and embraced her and she turned around to embrace him too. He wrapped his arms around her and they kissed. His damp curls dripped on her neck and down her back. He was dressed in nothing; she only in a long men's t-shirt. He reached beneath her shirt, not with probing hands, but just to feel the bare skin, and they kissed once more.

It was a searching kiss, a kiss with a question mark in it. Khalid's question was simple enough: should we make love now or drink the coffee first? This was a tough choice for someone so devoted to his morning coffee.

Her question, however, was a lingering one, filled with fearful doubts of every size and shape. She kissed him back, but it hurt her and she did not even know why. It hurt in her throat, and behind her eyes. Every part of her body felt constricted with a subdued, inexplicable rage.

Khalid's kisses on her lips then her neck and her shoulders awakened in her no sexual desire, but rather the desire to pinch him as hard as she could. She felt an irrational urge swelling under her skin—the urge to hurt him once for every time he had hurt her, and to hurt him twice for every time she had been injured by others before him.

A sword rose swiftly into Irene's throat as Khalid slipped his fingers under her shirt to touch her breast. She longed desperately for good things, but she was tormented by the fear that she had already lost the path back to him and to herself. She suppressed the urge to draw blood from his back with her fingernails, but it was useless to try to make love in the war zone that her heart had become.

I hate you, Irene blurted out in a choked hiss. She was shocked at the words that had spilled out on their own.

Khalid looked at her as if she had thrust a knife through his heart. He dropped his arms quickly from her body. And as he did so, the whole breakfast tray—coffee, sugar, fruit, cookies, came crashing to the bathroom floor.

With his finger always on the pulse of the moment, Khalid knew what was at stake when he spoke:

You're hopeless, he said, indifferent to the broken pile of cups and dishes. Not the least bit concerned about the coffee running across the slanted floor, soaking into and darkening the small mound of sugar at his feet, he added, *Sometimes, I think you're hopeless.*

The inclusion of this small qualifier was like a tiny ornamental window: just large enough for Irene to peer through, but not wide enough for her to climb out, in either direction.

8
Our Tent, Our Star

There's a lone man sitting in the sand. His feet are bare and dipped in the Pacific Ocean. Waves come and go, washing his feet with white foam. Above him he spies a seagull hovering overhead. He whispers: *I told you about the Red Sea, the Dead Sea, and the sand. I told you about the Sea of Galilee, and thyme dancing on the mountains. I told you about the river and the music, and the smell of carob in the morning. Then I told you about The End.*

I just wanted you to know how it felt to live with no horizon, but the horizon of sorrow. How can we travel together when you are tossed about on gusts of wind and I am trapped in a land where I am a stranger? Are we connected only by the salty air between us? Are we connected by anything other than mere chance?

There were years in Khalid's life that he preferred not to think or talk about at all, the years that he didn't even count as part of his life: when everything crumbled around him, and he began to understand words like war, exile, despair. He began to know that there was no refuge, no resting place for him in this world.

There were certain things that never failed to make him travel to other selves, to other places and times in his mind.

One was a poem called "Beirut" by Mahmoud Darwish. Another was a favorite Fairouz song:

What remains of the stories?
What remains of the trees?
What remains of the streets?
What remains of the nights?

What remains of love?
Of conversations? Of laughter?
Of tears?

What remains?
What remains, beloved?
Little stories scattered by the wind.

Irene had been hearing bits and fragments of Khalid's stories over the three years they had been together. He told her about the delights of a boyhood in East Jerusalem—the freedom of wandering for hours in the hills, trapping birds, playing hide and seek with friends. She heard stories about Aunt Salwa and how her gentle strength had saved him from ruin. She knew about his fateful confrontation with the soldiers, and about his sudden deportation. And about his one good year in Beirut before the civil war erupted. In that glimmering city by the sea, when he was still known as Sayeed, he had known a brief moment of repose.

In 1974 when he was cast on the Jordanian border with no passport, no money, and no food, it was the beginning of a new life. Sayeed found himself alone on the outskirts of Amman with nowhere to go. He had always been resourceful, but the only useful thing he now carried with him was a pocketful of memories.

The first thing he remembered was his Aunt Salwa's

stories about her own Aunt Mary, Uncle Aisa, and their daughters, who became refugees in 1948 in Beirut. Salwa visited them once in the late fifties with Sayeed's father and mother, before Sayeed was born. Salwa always spoke with affection of her cousins in Beirut, and the beauty of the city itself. So on that first morning in Jordan, Sayeed knew that he would seek out his family in Lebanon.

He worked for a week lifting boxes out of trucks in Amman until he had earned bus fare through Damascus and on to Lebanon. When the bus arrived at the Syrian border, they took him down and stopped him from crossing, because he had no official papers. He slept overnight in the customs house on a folding chair. Finally in the morning the two guards took pity on him; they woke him with half of a sandwich and a glass of hot tea with mint leaves in it. They realized that he wasn't going anywhere, in fact had nowhere to go. And so after feeding him, the soldiers quietly nodded him across the checkpoint. From there he hitchhiked his way to the city. By the time he finally arrived in Beirut, he was worn out with exhaustion and hunger.

As he dragged his worn body through the streets of Beirut, Salwa's hands appeared before him, offering warm bread, saying, *Be strong, Sayeed, be brave*. It was the bread that he longed for at that moment, not her hands, or her words. Just bread, crusty on the outside, soft and yeasty inside, its pores filled with steam.

He was still wearing the same dirty school clothes—the white shirt and blue pants that he'd been wearing since he was deported. He daydreamed of finding his cousins, and of the food they might serve if he found them—vegetable stews, stuffed grape leaves, loads of rice piled high with lamb and nuts...everything he missed from home. Food was the only thing on his mind as he trudged through the refugee camps in search of some remnants of his father's family.

In a street café in Shatila he stopped next to two old men smoking water pipes and drinking coffee from little white cups. Their earthen faces, care-worn and warm, reminded him of the old men of Jerusalem. He came close to them and asked if they'd heard of his cousins. He noticed immediately that they spoke in a familiar accent.

The kid's looking for dar Aseelah from Safad. Have you heard of this family? one man spoke into the ear of the other who seemed to be hard of hearing. The other man, wearing a white *hattah* with a black cord around it, exhaled a long breath of cooled smoke. *Dar Aseelah, strange name. Are you sure they're from Safad?* He paused and looked over his shoulder. *Ya Hassan,* he called loudly into the owner of the café, *ever heard of an Aseelah family?* The café man walked over to the table drying his hands on a dingy towel. *Aseelah...Aseelah...*he muttered shaking his head. *Are you sure they're in Beirut, not down South in Ein al-Hilweh?* Sayeed was confused by all these names and this new city, bustling all around him.

Poor thing, he's tired, said the first old man with concern. *Sit down,* he told the boy. *What's your name, son?* he asked, pulling up a chair. *Sayeed,* he said quietly. *Welcome, Sayeed,* the man said and clapped him on the shoulder. Then he called out to a child playing across the alley. *Come here, boy!* He pulled some money from his pocket and placed it in the hand of his grandson who had arrived quickly by his side. *Run and buy our guest here a sandwich.* Then he turned to Sayeed. *What would you like, boss? Falafel, shawarma? No need to be shy. We're all one big family here.*

Sayeed didn't say a word. Everything he had been taught about manners prevented him from asking for food. To indicate a preference between shawarma and falafel would be as good as placing an order. A lump swelled in his throat; he was in dangerous proximity to tears. *I'm not really hungry*, he said as casually as he could, *I just ate.* The old man smiled with a knowing look, clucked his tongue and shook his head. He shooed his grandson along, saying, *go on, make it falafel with everything on it and get him a cola too.*

With each bite of the sandwich, Sayeed's mind cleared and lost the bleary stains of his last hours and days. His head filled with a warm sensation. He became almost chipper, telling these men how he had arrived from a village near Jerusalem. *They kicked me out,* he told them, *threw me out because I didn't put up with their crap. I don't regret it.*

I'll tell you what, said the old man, Abu Ali. *You can come home with me and stay with my family until you find yours. We don't have much space, but at least you will have somewhere to go.* Sayeed nodded and said thanks.

The old man shook his head solemnly and repeated a well-known maxim: *No thanks are needed for a duty fulfilled.*

In a few minutes Abu Ali, with his long *galabiya* and cane, was escorting Sayeed through the narrow streets of the Shatila refugee camp. The tents had been replaced by cinderblock buildings constructed without planning or code. It was a miserable shantytown of low structures with corrugated tin roofs and ad hoc electrical wiring. Water and even sewage trickled down the gutters through the unpaved streets. The dirty walls were plastered with PLO posters, some mourning martyrs, some advertising the latest attempts at a health or sanitation project. Along the way Sayeed saw several young men with machine guns hanging across their chests.

Those are our fedayeen, the old man told him, noticing Sayeed's interest. *Someday they will liberate our land and then we'll all return to Palestine, insha'Allah.* Sayeed was astonished at how young they were, some even his own age.

Can anyone join them? he asked the old man. Abu Ali let out a sad little chuckle, a chuckle that was reminiscent of his own Aunt Salwa's weary laugh. With that, the old man lifted his cane and pointed to a small two-room hut with a piece of blue metal in place of a door. *Aywa. Here we are,* he said in English, *It is not Haifa, but what we shall do? What we shall do?* This was his English left over from the old days of British rule in Palestine. All the old men walked around with a few of these phrases tucked away on their tongues.

Sayeed was about to cross the threshold to a new life. He looked hesitantly at the creaking makeshift door. *Don't be worried, son,* said the old man in Arabic again, pushing the blue door with his cane. *God is merciful. God will provide.*

That afternoon, Abu Ali's twin grandsons, Bilal and Naseem, came from school and found that they had a new guest in their home. They were a year older than Sayeed, and were excited to have a new companion dropped into their midst. Their mother prepared a modest snack of bread, olives, and yogurt cheese, and the boys hit it off right away.

After their meal, they invited Sayeed to play soccer with some of their other friends. Though tired and sleepy, Sayeed agreed to go along with them. Before the game started, the boys all crowded around, asking Sayeed questions about his arrival in Beirut. Before Sayeed could say anything, Bilal piped in: *Sayeed's a hero. Let him tell you about getting kicked out of Palestine.*

Sayeed told them the details about the incident at the village well. And as he looked into the faces of this ragtag collection of kids, refugees who still looked and talked just like him, he felt at home. In their tanned, dirt-smudged faces, he saw the reflections of the playmates that he had just left behind. It was an eerie feeling, to find a Palestinian town in the heart of Lebanon. On his first day in Beirut, he was already accepted as one of them.

For their part, Bilal, Naseem, and their friends, who were born in the camps, were impressed with Sayeed. Having had the privilege of being born in Palestine, Sayeed was seen as somehow smarter, wiser, more "authentic." They grew up hearing stories of places like Safouriyeh, Haifa, Acre, and Tiberias; Sayeed represented the living, breathing reminder of all of these unseen places.

Over the next few days the twins' grandfather was putting

the word out about Sayeed's search for his family. In the meantime, Bilal and Naseem began to introduce Sayeed to life in the camps. They were proud to show Sayeed the tricks of the trade, the ins and the outs, the do's and the don'ts of survival in the streets. *Your best bet in the camps*, they told him, *is to join Fatah,* they said. *In the meantime, watch your back.*

Born barefoot and penniless, Bilal and Naseem lived with the mad enthusiasm of those who know that their future is already written. *Maktoub*, as they say. They were always full of pranks and jokes. One minute they were swiping a handful of roasted pistachios from a nut vendor, the next minute they were scooping a baby from its mother's lap, tossing it in the air, smothering it with coos and kisses. Of course, they knew where all the pretty girls lived in Sabra and Shatila, and pretended they were well acquainted with them.

Bilal and Naseem were not identical twins; in fact they were almost opposites. Bilal was dark-skinned, had a crop of thick kinky hair, a broad face, and a wide fleshy nose. His facial expression alternated between a look of profound existential confusion and the conspiratorial air of someone who is suppressing a gale of laughter. Other kids were drawn to him, perhaps if only to find out what the hidden joke was.

Bilal's brother Naseem was light-skinned, tall and thin. He walked around with a tilted offhand smile on his lips and a bend in his knee. He had a wiry frame, always either moving or poised on the edge of movement. It was from Naseem, a budding musician and *oud* player, that Sayeed picked up his lifelong habit of rubbing his palms together. This was Naseem's best-known gesture; it was as if his whole being emanated the warning: *I'm ready for anything.*

Friendship and camaraderie suddenly seemed to Sayeed like a fair compensation for everything that had ever happened to him. The sea of tears behind his eyes made his friends appear in a glittering golden halo. Though he had always been quiet and serious, their bravado mirrored and made light of the rage in him. The three of them became immediately inseparable. They took him to their UNRWA school, for walks, to play soccer, and to play at the beach. The first days of his arrival in Beirut were, in his own memory, the best moments of his life.

Within a few days, however, Abu Ali succeeded in locating the Aseelah family. They were living on the outskirts of an entirely different camp, Tel Zaatar, on the edge of East Beirut. Bilal and Naseem's grandfather found the phone number, called them, and explained everything to the Aseelah grandmother. Naturally, she knew of Sayeed's existence and said she was delighted to take him in.

Sayeed was nervous as he listened to Abu Ali's discussion with his great aunt, Mary. He had never met this side of the family. He already felt at home with Bilal and Naseem. It embarrassed him to think that he was going to impose himself again on another set of strangers.

Don't worry, Abu Ali smiled gently, *they're good people, praise God.*

The next day, Sayeed, Bilal and Naseem caught a special service taxi across town. His two friends agreed to accompany him to his relatives' house. They scratched around in their pockets for change and jumped into the backseat of the taxi with glee.

Aaaah, look at that fine girl walking down the street, said Naseem rubbing his palms together and then shaking them out again. *Oh, it's just Hiba,* laughed Bilal when the taxi passed her by, *not much hope there.*

Who's to say? grinned Naseem. *Who's to say what I might have already done while you were busy daydreaming.* He smiled and clapped them both on the back.

They joked and bantered all the way across town, as they jumped out of one taxi, waited for the next, took it further, then found a third to take them the rest of the way to Tel

Zaatar. At the edge of the camp the three of them skipped arm in arm, until they found the location of Sayeed's relatives.

The Aseelah house was bigger than any other in the area. Its two stories were built of actual stone, rather than cinder blocks, and it was encircled by an iron gate with railings leading up the stairs to the door. Sayeed took a deep breath and heaved a nervous sigh.

Do you want us to come in with you? asked Bilal.

Of course, said Sayeed. They knocked and waited, uneasy. In front of such a well-kept house they felt like tramps.

Sayeed's paternal grandfather, also named Sayeed, had a younger sister Mary. In the late thirties, Mary married a businessman from Safad, named Aisa al-Aseelah. Aisa met Mary on one of his trips to Jerusalem, married her, and brought her North to Safad, a beautiful town in the mountains of Galilee. Aisa owned a clothing shop and a general store. He was also a self-educated art collector. The locals gently mocked his interest in ancient calligraphy, but he made regular trips to Damascus, Cairo, and Baghdad to acquire the artifacts in his private collection.

Mary gave birth to two daughters, Christine and Lydia, born only a year apart, in 1944 and 1945. When the town fell in 1948, the family was marched at gunpoint out of town. They fled to the border with nothing but two suitcases full of clothes, Mary's jewelry, and the keys and deeds to their home and businesses. They intended to return when the war was over. In a week or two, they expected.

Within two weeks, however, a Jewish sculptor originally from Austria acquired their large stone house from the Israeli housing office for next to nothing. It was still furnished with all the Aseelah's personal items, including Aisa's calligraphy collection, which the sculptor sold many years later at auction in London for more than a million British sterling. The

Aseelah living room, with its lovely stone and tile work, was transformed into a luxurious art studio with an abundance of natural light.

Twice the Aseelah family tried to cross the border to return to Palestine, only to be turned back. The father, Aisa, tried to use his many business connections to arrange some kind of special deal, to no avail. Later, when the full scope of their tragedy was known, Aisa bitterly repeated that he would rather have died like a dog by the side of the road in Palestine than live out his days in exile.

After a year of suffering and waiting, and relying on UN food rations to feed their children, Aisa finally sold his wife's dowry jewelry and set up a small business in Tel Zaatar. Within three years he had built up a thriving shop in Hamra, the premier shopping district in downtown Beirut.

Aisa and Mary were among the lucky few. Most of their compatriots were peasants, and without land in Lebanon they became utterly destitute. But by the late fifties, Aisa and Mary managed to buy several apartments and an office building that they rented out. And though Aisa could have moved his family away from the Tel Zaatar camp and into the more comfortable Lebanese suburbs, he did not. Instead he built this fine house on the outskirts of the camp. He had always said that he didn't want to forget where he came from. He never gave up on the dream of one day returning to the home he had built with his own hands in Safad.

On the day of the 1967 Arab defeat, Aisa died of a heart attack. The family business passed into the hands of his oldest daughter Christine and her husband, Moussa. And now in the well-appointed stone house in that otherwise wretched camp of Tel Zaater lived Christine and Moussa, their infant son George, Lydia, who remained unmarried, and Sitti Mary, Sayeed's grandfather's sister.

Sayeed knew almost nothing about this branch of the family, except what he had heard from his Aunt Salwa over the years. Remembering these stories, and remembering Abu

Ali's words, *they're good people,* gave Sayeed courage as he knocked on the wooden door. While he waited, he studied the lovely calligraphic inscription above the entryway: *Peace to All Who Enter Here.*

It was Sitti Mary, a woman in her late fifties, wearing a white kerchief and a flowered dress, who opened the door. She immediately pulled Sayeed inside, pulling his face to hers for several warm kisses. *Ahlain, ahlain habibi! You look just like my nephew, Hanna, God rest his soul.* She rushed him into the foyer. His two friends followed bashfully behind.

The house was spacious, clean, immaculate. Bilal and Naseem, whose father was a worker, had never set foot inside a house with high ceilings and oil paintings on the walls, ceramic statuettes on the side tables. The boys stood back while Sayeed's two older cousins came rushing down the hallway—one, a tall pretty woman, was holding a baby in her arms.

I'm Christine. And this is my sister Lydia. Say hello to Sayeed, George, Christine cooed into the baby's little ear, wiggling his fingers at Sayeed. Sayeed patted the baby's hand and said Hello to him, then looked up and repeated himself shyly. *Hello,* he smiled to his beaming relatives. Sitti Mary guided her grandnephew into the living room and Lydia went to get refreshments. Bilal and Naseem came and sat down too, but didn't say a word. They felt ashamed of their scuffed, ill-fitting shoes and their hand-me-down clothes. The Christian icons and the cross on the walls also made them feel out of place.

Thanks for bringing Sayeed here, Christine turned to the two brothers. Like a master telling her servant, *That will be all for now,* there was an unmistakable note of dismissal in her voice. At that point Lydia returned with a tray of lemonade and cookies, and as she served them she gave the boys a friendly wink to counter her sister's brusque demeanor.

Meanwhile Sayeed was being asked about his family, about Aunt Salwa, and about the events that had brought him to Beirut without money, clothes, or a place to stay.

Sayeed's a hero, Naseem chipped in, echoing his brother's words earlier that week. No one responded and Christine stared at him blankly. In a minute Naseem nudged his brother, indicating that they should leave. They both got up from the Italian couch and said goodbye at the same time. *We'll see you soon, right?* Bilal asked Sayeed. They felt as though they were leaving their new friend in a cold wilderness, a world that they would never be allowed to enter again. *You'll still come to see us tomorrow? Right?* Naseem asked. Sayeed walked them toward the door. *I'll come tomorrow,* he promised in a whisper.

Sayeed quickly became a part of the Aseelah family. They welcomed him as one of their own. It was a strange feeling— to be meeting people who would have been a regular part of his life had history not intervened. Sitti Mary and his own grandfather were sister and brother. His father and Aunt Salwa were first cousins to Christine and Lydia. It came as a surprise to Sayeed that Sitti Mary knew so much about his own village, Tel Zahara.

What do you think? she exclaimed. *I was born there! I was married and had two children before we were exiled. You children seem to think that the war of '48 is ancient history!*

Sitti Mary would then tell Sayeed more things that he did not know, such as the fact that her brother, his grandfather, had been arrested by the British in the revolt in the mid-thirties. *He didn't wind up on the British gallows,* she said, *but others did.*

Mary also revealed personal anecdotes, such as the fact that his mother, Halima, was offered a scholarship to study in London. *She was a gifted young lady, your mother,* Sitti

Mary told him, *but in those days it was unheard of for a girl to travel abroad to study. So she got married to your father instead And gave birth to you, of course.* Sitti Mary's voice trailed off as she added the words, *God rest her soul.*

Within a week of his arrival, Sayeed began to work at the family store downtown. He helped Moussa and Christine by doing odd jobs, running errands, and some bookkeeping. As she watched Sayeed's charming way with the customers, and his eagle-eye for mistakes in the books, Christine soon understood what a brilliant, well-bred young cousin she had. She was not at all displeased with his appearance on the scene and planned to enroll him at a private school in Ashrafiyeh in the fall.

With her entrepreneurial spirit, Christine was already preparing to groom Sayeed for assimilation into middle-class Lebanese society. She had it all planned out. He would study at the American University, become a lawyer or an engineer, marry a nice Christian Lebanese girl, take vacations in Paris and the French Riviera, and become a shining example of a talented Palestinian who would be "a credit to his people."

In Christine's mind, the only hitch in the plan was Sayeed's ongoing friendship with Bilal and Naseem. For her, who had begun to think of herself as Lebanese, these boys typified all that was wrong with the Palestinians of the camps. Their very presence was an ominous signifier, a reminder of destitution, ignorance, and potential trouble. In Bilal's dark face she envisioned the shadows of future turbulence. In Naseem's supple limbs she saw the wretched of the earth poised for militant action.

They'll wind up as troublemakers, she would often say. Christine's sister Lydia wholeheartedly disagreed with this perspective. *Just because Baba was successful, doesn't make us better. Shame on you,* Lydia scolded her older sister.

Regardless of what anyone thought, Bilal and Naseem remained fiercely loyal to Sayeed. Even when they came to realize that Sayeed would lead a more privileged life in Beirut than they, it didn't matter. They considered Sayeed as one of them. And Sayeed was equally loyal. Whatever pocket money he earned at the store was shared with his friends. Whatever special treat Lydia and Sitti Mary might cook—rolled grape leaves, date cakes, and pastries—Sayeed would put some aside for the twins.

The three of them, plus a few more boys, organized a secret club together. The first goal of the club was to scrape, steal, and stash whatever money they could—to buy Naseem his own oud. They kept the money in an old jar that they buried with much stealth in an empty lot. After several months of saving, they finally managed to go to the store and purchase the least expensive instrument. With the left over money they bought a bottle of cheap brandy and got drunk at the beach. Naseem serenaded them with tunes by Abd al-Wahad and Farid al-Atrache that he had already learned on borrowed instruments. They felt that they were finally living the good life. Things could only get better and better.

In the coming year, they trapped birds together, played tag in the streets, talked politics, and cursed out loud, testing their ability to sound tough and fearless. They went to the Corniche in the evenings to escape the oppressive squalor that enveloped them in the camps. And on the beach facing the western sunset, they always found time to play.

They were children on the edge of manhood, so they played at being men. They played make-believe—make-believe love and make-believe wars and make-believe power. Make-believe manhood. But they didn't know the price that manhood was going to exact from them—before they had even had a chance to finish being children.

9

The Homeland behind Our Eyes

There are two black spots behind Khalid's eyes where even sleep never manages to reach. As hard as he tries. They are not composed of memories or images or the gentle play of shadow and light. In essence they are nothing, and yet they are there.

Music makes them dance. Poetry makes them hide. But only love and laughter make them disappear for a time. In his dreams they take the form of his father and mother, knocking on his door.

Why did you come? he asks them in a heavy voice. *Because we need you*, they respond. They call him by name— *Sayeed*—and guide him halfway through the door to the bakery. Everything is broken, in ruins. There are strangers working behind the ovens, people he doesn't recognize at all. His voice echoes as if in an empty cathedral, *Mama? Baba?* but they have already gone.

Two black spots hover between consciousness and its opposite. Not hovering, but rather suspended—moving, yet residential—the way Khalid says the sea is: *moving, yet residential.*

Khalid thinks of becoming a painter some day to claim the color behind his eyes, the homeland behind his eyes, the two dark spots made only of absence and loss. In his dreams they take the form of Bilal and Naseem. They are leaning casually against a wall in Tel Zaatar, smiling.

Flowers? Don't bring us any more flowers, they say.

They crack sunflower seeds between their teeth, tossing the shells on the dusty ground. They are whitewashing the graffiti on a crumbling wall in Shatila. The wall is falling apart before their eyes, but they keep whitewashing just the same. Up and down, up and down.

Flowers? they ask again, bewildered at the way their own voices fade to silence.

Khalid will wake to find that Bilal and Naseem are not there. He finds himself instead in an unfamiliar room. *Where am I?* he wonders for an instant that seems to last forever. Then he hears the cry of the Mexican vegetable-seller through the window calling, *Tomaaaaatos, Avocados, Eggs. Tomaaaaatos, Avocados, and Eggs.* This familiar morning call of the neighborhood produce vendor allows him to recognize the whole apparatus of facts that constitute his present moment; and he releases the heavy sigh that accompanies a full, detailed comprehension of the certainties of his life:

No, I'm not in Beirut anymore. I'm in California. Bilal and Naseem are not here with me. It's Saturday morning. I lie next to Irene. I am angry with her. And a war is brewing in Iraq.

Much has happened in the outside world in the past year. A new Republican has been elected President. Panama has been invaded as a Christmas present to docile voters. The Soviet Union and the whole Eastern Bloc have recently collapsed like a house of straw.

For Khalid these political happenings are not distant, abstract events. He takes them very personally, feels that his very soul and the souls of everyone around him are deeply affected by these immense changes. Khalid is not encouraged, to say the least, that the world will now be ruled by one superpower.

Now a new war is looming on the horizon and Khalid feels poisoned by the hawkish language, the yellow ribbons on all the trees, the legions of spokespeople who inhabit the television screens on prime time every day. He feels injured by the "reasonable" voices of Pentagon experts talking about his part of the world. He is wounded by the sharp faces of think tank researchers who discuss the potential effects of a mid-east oil war on "Israel's ability to contain the Palestinian Intifada."

But the Intifada—that's a word that lights a fire in Khalid's spirit. This uprising of Palestinian youth represents the manifestation of all Khalid's favorite philosophies. A stone aimed directly at the occupier's tank is the simple yet eloquent incarnation of Marx's dialectical materialism. A homemade slingshot twirling masterfully above the head of a child is Trotsky's permanent revolution. The ambushes and roadblocks created from burning tires are Nietzsche's joy of destruction. It has been a long time since Khalid felt such a renewed sense of purpose.

Every day for the past year, Khalid has set up an information table on campus to hand out brochures and leaflets. With the patience and zeal of a religious convert, he informs everyone within earshot about the entire modern history of the Middle East.

Have you heard of the Balfour declaration? He asks a young student chewing gum and strolling past. *The Sykes-Picot Agreement?* She keeps walking. *Would you like to know?* She shakes her head.

Do you know where your tax dollars go? Khalid calls out loudly to the next batch of students walking towards him.

When it's time to say goodnight to his friends—after a dinner or an evening together—he always says goodnight in the new post-Intifada way: *May you wake up to a homeland!* It's a line from a poem by his favorite poet Mahmoud Darwish that has been set to music by a popular Lebanese singer. Khalid plays the tape incessantly, morning, noon, and night.

But the Intifada has brought terrible news as well: Aunt Salwa herself was even arrested by the Israelis for allowing some stone-throwing boys to take refuge in her house. In prison she was kept standing in a dark closet for three days. When she still told them nothing, they finally let her go, knowing already that she really had nothing to tell.

Salwa often calls Khalid in the middle of the night to offer the latest news of demonstrations and arrests from Tel Zahara, which is not a village anymore, but a part of sprawling East Jerusalem. Khalid also calls her regularly to check on her safety, and to confirm rumors and news reports.

Whereas the uprising has been giving Khalid a new sense of urgency, this new "stand-off" in the Persian Gulf has altogether changed that interior landscape. The pre-war atmosphere that has soaked into every pore of daily life has embittered Khalid more than humanly imaginable. Peter Jennings, Dan Rather, and Ted Koppel have become an integral part of Khalid's private life. He sustains intimate, one-sided conversations with them every night in his living room.

Filled with all of these thoughts, Khalid turns over to look at Irene sleeping next to him; and he's riddled with yet more discordant feelings. He sighs out loud. Sometimes he wonders if she is even capable of love. She always seems to be pulling away from him, keeping her distance, staying safe. He senses that she is permanently receding beyond his reach. *Am I too harsh on her?* he wonders. *Maybe,* he thinks, *but she hasn't even tried to fix things between us. She keeps her thoughts to herself.*

He still desires her, wants to wake her and hold her and share with her whatever goodness remains in him. Recalling the pleasures of Irene's body makes him think of figs, ripe and purple, splitting at their seams. Her love brings him to the sensations of his childhood.

Long ago in a time almost before memory, he walked hand in hand with his grandfather to the olive grove in springtime. He was just a small boy, so close to the ground he could smell the earth and stones beneath his feet. Tiny sparrows darted amongst red poppies that had bloomed over the hillside. His grandfather lifted him high up into the tree and showed him an olive branch. His grandfather told him, *There is nothing here now, do you see? But by the end of the summer, the branches will be filled with fruit. Whatever is invisible eventually becomes visible again.*

When Khalid lies in Irene's arms, he sometimes feels that he can smell that same earth again, and hear his grandfather's words, and hear the sparrows scratching among the red poppies.

But today, no, he's too angry to believe in the invisible becoming visible again. All he can see right now is death, not life. He and Irene had another fight the night before. Khalid's head rolls with an injection of fresh pain. The problem is that Irene will never admit that she can be wrong. She's stubborn and cold and...*white.* White, not as a color, but rather a mentality, an inborn cultural arrogance that makes her blind to other ways of acting, perceiving, thinking about the world. He hadn't always been so sensitive to this trait, but now, lately, especially with the war fever spreading everywhere, it's all he can see anymore.

In her childhood, Irene's parents created a shelter in the paralyzed center of a world governed by money and social rules. She had been raised in a universe that considered itself superior to everyone else. Her family would probably never admit their assumption of superiority over black or brown people. But it was there; this was the poison bubble Irene had grown in. It wasn't just the privilege, it wasn't just the complacency, it wasn't just the spiritual emptiness that had spoiled her. It was racism that had damaged Irene the most. But was it Khalid's JOB to put up with it?

Khalid could see her wounds, the wounds of trying to change, to escape, to become a whole human. And he could accept this…if only she didn't freeze up on him, if only she didn't turn her arrogance against him, knowingly.

Recalling the conflict engendered by this struggle between them is enough to send Khalid hurtling away from her this morning. Khalid slips from the bed and pulls on some jeans and walks out of the bedroom to the kitchen of their cottage.

There are certain rituals that give Khalid pleasure, a pleasure that does not override the presence of pain, but which modulates it, adding structure and definition to it. One of those rituals is the preparation of Arabic coffee in the morning. Khalid begins to prepare for this ceremony with the studied manners of a high priest, selecting the ingredients from the cupboard with somber poise. Preparing his coffee meticulously, Khalid observes certain rules that he himself invented, and which have become, therefore, axiomatic:

- Rinse the dirty coffeepot, never wash
- Fill coffeepot 2/3 full of water, even if only one person is drinking
- Add heaping, ambiguous amounts of coffee and sugar after water boils
- Never (ever) stir coffee with spoon; let the boiling action mix coffee
- Always let it boil over the top (like a revolution)
- Offer it to everyone in the vicinity, friend or foe

The last point on this list of rules is the key to Khalid's personality.

Behind every fact in Khalid's life there is a counter-fact to counteract the first fact.

In a moment of wrath, Khalid is ever able to remember Aunt Salwa, who nourished him with stories and fruit as a child. Yet in a moment of tenderness, he is unable to purge the image of the soldier who spat in his childhood's water. In a moment of despair, Khalid hears the tender echoes of Beethoven's sonatas. Yet in the echoes of Beethoven he is able to hear the lingering clamor of Napoleon's armies conquering Europe.

He openly denounces the meaninglessness of an intelligentsia which has forgotten how to organize, unite, and act, but then he himself will lock the bedroom door for two whole weeks in order to finish reading both *Anna Karenina* and *War and Peace* one after the other.

He hates and decries the fact that other men are attracted to Irene and that she thrives on their attention. But at the same time he secretly enjoys the erotic potential it brings to their bed.

He is resentful of Irene's background, but when remnants of her private school upbringing emerge in useful ways—such as her ability to be the house dictionary, encyclopedia, and memory bank all rolled in one—he is again ready to embrace her contradictions.

As Khalid pours himself coffee in the kitchen, he mentally reviews Irene's transgressions of the night before. *She is so bloody stubborn*, he thinks, *stubborn!* Then, just as he is about to take his first sip of coffee, he hears her footsteps in the doorway behind him. And despite all of his angry feelings, he pours Irene a small cup of coffee and offers it to her when she enters the kitchen.

Finjan ahwe? he asks in Arabic in a neutral tone that expresses grudging displeasure, as if to say, *I offer you this coffee in spite of my best instincts.*

Without even a thoughtful pause, Irene responds, *Laa. Shukran*, also in Arabic. No thanks. And that's all it takes. Khalid places the cup on the counter coldly and brushes past her silently. To him, her refusal of his coffee represents an open rejection of him, and a rejection of the olive branch that he has extended.

He walks briskly out the door of the cottage and plants himself on the front cement stoop. Lighting a cigarette, he begins to brood. Even as a little green-headed hummingbird sucks the nectar from a nearby orange trumpet flower, even as the morning sunlight dances on the extravagant bird-of-paradise blooms across the courtyard, Khalid remains oblivious to all external evidence of beauty. He is magnetized, drawn to the extreme poles of his existence—anger and grief. Whatever shades of emotion lie in between these two permanent fixtures remain inaccessible.

There are two black spots behind Khalid's eyes where consolation can never be found.

Sometimes these black spots take the form of an endless void that he could swim in forever. Three times he has pulled himself from that bottomless abyss. The first time was the night he found himself alone by the side of the road in a refugee camp in Jordan. On that night he was saved by the wailing sound of the mijwiz. When it flared up and lit the night with its electric echoes, he was able to shinny up the side of its notes and feel almost triumphant, almost free.

The second time was in Beirut in the middle of the civil war, a war that shattered everything in his life. He called the next two years "the dead years," and to this day he doesn't count them as part of his life.

The third time was in London right after the Israeli invasion of Beirut. He left a week after the massacres in the camps. Sarah was bringing him to the U.S. and he stopped for a month in London to visit an old friend, Hussein. On his first night, they held a dinner party in his honor in Wimbledon. There was a lot of drinking and laughter and disco music. He felt like a walking corpse in a graveyard of corpses. Donna Summer was playing loudly, shrieks of laughter echoed off the white walls. A British girl in a mini-skirt was spinning like a green and yellow top. Khalid looked up across the room and caught his friend's eye. He lunged over to him and clung tightly to his wool sweater. *Husseeiiiin,* he cried into his ear, *they want us to diiiie!*

What was it that could have pulled him from that despair? At that moment Hussein stopped the party. He turned off the music, asked the guests to all be quiet, and began to recite a poem for everyone. The poem was Tawfiq Zayyad's legendary "I Call to You," a poem that almost every Arab could recite by heart. And when Khalid looked out at the faces in the room then, he felt suddenly that he was now swimming in a sea of love rather than despair.

It was that night that Khalid decided to change his name from Sayeed to Khalid. For he resolved that he would resist death in all its forms. Rather than live on as "The Happy One" he would now become "Eternal."

We will change our names, he whispered to himself. *We will live in exile. But we will not die.*

But that was then. Even in 1982 it was still really the tail end of the seventies. Now, it's the beginning of the nineties, and Khalid feels that there is no rope to pull him up and out of this present darkness.

Here in California there is nothing on which to grasp. The surfaces are all polished. The rhetoric—circular and repetitive. The newscasters and politicians, neighbors, and even professors are all so smooth, wearing deceptive masks of civility, liberality, and benevolence. What are these masks hiding? Lately, he finds that he recognizes no one here. And no one recognizes him. In short, he is a stranger, sliding downwards into the void. Sometimes he sees Irene as just one part of a frightening masquerade.

It's only 9 a.m., California time, but Khalid is already mentally exhausted. After finishing his coffee, he walks silently past Irene again, and collapses on the couch in the living room. She disappears into the bedroom, purposefully avoiding his wrenching gloom. Instead of doing the things they enjoy together—writing, listening to music, cooking, taking walks in the park, talking, reading—they will spend this whole Saturday in silence, avoiding each other like two repellent magnets.

From where he reclines, he sees the luminous fruit bowl sitting innocently on the counter. Three yellow bananas jut out of the top of the bowl, a beacon of absurdity and futility. The bananas flash their silly half-moon smiles, mocking the excess of his feelings. Staring at those three pieces of fruit, Khalid feels a sense of vertigo and nausea as he calls to mind the whole episode the night before that brought him to this present moment of desolation.

10
Story of a Banana

It was Friday evening. Irene and Khalid came home from campus together after class, and Mounir stopped by for an impromptu cup of coffee. He planned to stay for an hour, but ended up staying all evening. The three of them sat around the kitchen, drinking coffee and discussing the situation in Kuwait and Iraq. These types of gatherings had become a regular event for Khalid, Irene, Mounir, Kathy, and other friends, including Sarah, who now lived alone. It was part of the daily routine to explicate every new speech, every report or newspaper article that appeared in print, every sign that war was coming sooner rather than later. Nothing was sacred and everything was an outrage.

When Mounir arrived with a bag of freshly roasted coffee beans, the stage was set.

After he had made and served the coffee, Khalid immediately mentioned an opinion piece he'd seen in the newspaper suggesting that this was precisely the opportune moment for the use of tactical nuclear weapons. According to Khalid, the columnist was arguing that since the government has already invested so much money in producing nuclear weapons, "we might as well use them."

Khalid was infuriated.

Well, you are dealing with an apocalyptic nation here, Irene said. *This country was founded on religious zealotry.*

And genocide, added Mounir.

Khalid interjected. *Where do you think Saddam even got his "weapons of mass destruction" from?* gesturing a set of quotation marks in the air as he spoke.

I know, I know, agreed Irene and Mounir nodding their heads.

When we were protesting Saddam, the U.S. was paying him. When we were crying out for help, they were arming him! Hypocrites!

They knew, Mounir added, *what a bastard he was. He was THEIR bastard.*

Irene, Khalid, and Mounir spent their entire evening drawing whole quarts of blood from this same political vein. Each took their turn to recount the most recent announcement, the most offensive linguistic gaffe. Anecdotes, jokes, and misquotes were used to underline political points.

They eventually traded the coffee for a bottle of whiskey, which made the harangue that much louder and more vehement. They traveled from the kitchen to the front stoop (to smoke and drink in the fresh air), then back to the kitchen for snacks, then into the living room to get comfortable so as to keep up the nonstop, scathing confab. Their drunken ruminations broadly encompassed global events and then descended into a fine-tuned analysis of the twitch in the Secretary of Defense's lower lip.

Every compulsive liar has an irrepressible tic, Khalid remarked. *In Dick Cheney's case it's that lip, that quivering, oscillating lower lip.*

Have you noticed it too? Irene squealed. *My god, it has a life of its own!*

That lip is desperately trying to scream out, "I'm lying! I'm lying!"

And have you guys noticed the names of these people? Mounir added, *DICK, COLON, and BUSH...oh my god.*

And don't forget SODOM, added Khalid.

They're planning an attack in the biblical sense... Irene laughed. They all got a bitter chuckle out of this, and many more jokes having to do with the relationship between war and sex were offered in quick succession. They had already downed most of the whiskey. Irene had been mixing hers with Coke, Khalid and Mounir were having it straight up.

It was late when Khalid took out a poem that he had written. He began to read it to Irene and Mounir:

> *America, America.*
> *Turn off your TV, America. We need to talk....*

Mounir interrupted Khalid, saying, *Talking? Now, to America, that would imply some kind of submissive impulse... no, not submissive...what's the word, Irene?*

Subservient? Irene offered. *Masochistic? Homoerotic?* Mounir shook his head.

Slow down, America, Khalid recited again with great drama and feeling. He was good at this. He drew out his words. He gestured grandly with liquid arms. His sonorous voice filled the room and the other two finally stopped talking.

> *In the dance of the dagger you cannot win.*
> *In the song of the eternal, you are an empty mall*
> *We are small, but our dreams are larger than smart bombs*
> *and our dignity and our children will survive.*

Ism'allah, Irene said when he finally finished. *Maybe you'll read it at the demo next weekend.*

What are you talking about? Khalid said, shaking his head defiantly. *I'm not going to any demonstration.* He upended the last shot of whiskey into his mouth, and slammed the glass on the table.

Why not? Irene asked. She felt the confrontational edge to his statement. Or rather she took the statement as confrontational because they had already made plans to go together. She was a member of the steering committee.

Because it's pointless. Your people WANT this war. His use of the word "your people" in this context was a sign of his growing irritation.

Then what was your whole poem about? Irene asked. *What's the point?*

I don't write poems to impress people, he said with accusation in his voice. *Just because I want to talk to America, doesn't mean America wants to talk to me.*

The tone had not yet reached a hostile pitch, but it contained the classic elements that could lead to open warfare. Mounir was not a stranger to their flare-ups and had often played moderator and "neutral third party." Although he too was drunk, he tried to defuse the tension.

Do you mind if I have a banana? Mounir asked in an overly casual voice, reaching for the fruit. *My blood sugar seems to be dropping.* On the counter behind Khalid there was a large bowl filled to the brim, crowned with three bananas. It was the mother of all fruit bowls.

Of course, said Khalid, leaning over to hand the banana to Mounir.

Actually, I'm saving those to make banana bread tomorrow, Irene interjected.

No big deal, Mounir said, *I'll have an orange instead.*

Banana bread? Khalid asked incredulously, slowing down the pace. *Banana bread?* he repeated again.

Yes, I've been craving it.

Well, can't you go to the store and get more bananas tomorrow?

I could, Irene said, *except that the bananas need to be very ripe. I've been saving these for a couple of days.*

Go ahead, Mounir, Khalid held out the banana to Mounir. *Whatever is ours is yours.* He spoke in Arabic as if to affirm the deeper connection that they shared.

"Laa, laa, laa," Mounir shook his head and protested.

That's fine. Let Irene make her bread, he switched back to English again.

I'll save you a big piece, Mounir, Irene added quasi-cheerfully. Although Khalid held the banana out again, Mounir didn't take it, and instead started to peel an orange.

Mmmm, I love oranges, Mounir grinned. *Oooh, this one is nice and sweet,* he said with a smile. *These can't be from Ralph's.* Neither Irene nor Khalid answered him.

It was too late for Mounir's lighthearted banter; the atmosphere was already mined with lethal energy. He tried to pull Khalid aside to convince him to calm down. But to no avail. The ill will in the room had reached the point that it was almost criminally negligent when Mounir got up and said that he had to go home.

As soon as he had departed, silence descended upon the house and there was nothing to prevent the two lovers from being pulled into a vortex of emptiness, with its inevitable downward pull.

Khalid disappeared immediately. He slipped off into the bedroom without a sound and without a word of goodnight. Irene walked around the cottage, pretending that it was absolutely critical to straighten up, clear dishes, and throw away the trash. She was hoping that Khalid would fall asleep before she came to bed. She finally went into the bedroom and climbed under the covers next to him. He was not asleep. She didn't even attempt to touch him or speak. They lay like that, side-by-side in the dark, for a long time.

Side by side they lay, frozen, choking with tension, not a seed of sympathy passing between them. Though Irene had been drinking too, she could smell the sour whiskey on his breath. A whole hour passed with each one waiting for the other to break the heavy silence. Finally Khalid's bitter voice penetrated the night:

I've figured you out, Irene.

Oh really? said Irene, bracing herself.

You are an opportunist.

This particular insult took Irene aback. *What did I do wrong?* she asked angrily.

He was silent and so she continued, *You must have some sort of special equipment for monitoring all my bad behavior.*

It doesn't take a high-tech device to register what an asshole you are.

I'd really like to know what the hell you are talking about.

There was silence again for a long moment. Irene did not know how to respond.

What the hell are you talking about? she repeated.

Pure egotists never see their own faults.

"*Kuss okhtak,*" Irene spat out in Arabic, a curse she had learned from him. *Would you stop it and tell me what this is all about?*

Khalid waited a second before he unveiled the indictment against her. *You are so thoughtless,* he exploded in what could have easily become a torrent of tears. *If a guest asks you for a banana, how do you dare refuse?*

Irene thought for a minute before responding, *Is that what this is all about? A banana?*

It's not about a banana; it's about you.

There were other fruits to eat. I don't see what's the big deal.

It's cheap—that's the big deal! Where I come from, we don't do shit like that. It's shameful!

Where I come from, we don't get so bent out of shape over a banana.

You all are so liberal here, Khalid replied. *Everything has the same exact value, which comes down to NO value whatsoever.*

They both paused, but Khalid jumped in more quickly than Irene.

Why do you offer someone an orange when they ask you for a banana? WHY? Don't you have any idea how rude you are?

Not half as rude as you're being right now, said Irene turning over, pretending to go to sleep.

Don't try to downplay the whole thing, Khalid said, grabbing her shoulder and turning her around.

I just can't believe this is happening, screeched Irene. *You are a nightmare, a fucking nightmare!*

Don't scream at me, you piece-of-shit whitey, he grabbed her shoulder again hard. She shielded her face. *Go ahead and make your banana bread.* He gripped her arm even tighter. *Go ahead and bomb the whole world to the Stone Age and pretend you are innocent,* he hissed in her face.

Get your hands off of me, she pushed him away and jumped out of bed and ran towards the door. *You're totally insane!* she shouted, slamming the door. *Insane,* she shouted through the door at him. *Insane,* she mumbled to herself as she stumbled about in the darkness.

Slam. That's the noise Khalid hears in his head as he now thinks about the fight. That's the way the fight ended, with the SLAM of the bedroom door. They had exchanged no other words until the moment he had offered, and Irene had rejected, his morning cup of coffee.

It used to be when he would fight with Irene, they made up before the night was through. But now they had carried it over into a second day. Irene finally came back to bed after he had already fallen asleep. And as he slept, Khalid made it a point not even to let their bodies brush against each other accidentally in the night.

It's still morning, and Khalid gazes across the room at the bananas in the fruit bowl on the counter. He feels betrayed by their bright, cheerful presence. He lifts himself off the couch and walks to the counter. Picking up all three bananas, he throws them straight into the trash.

Then he sinks back onto the couch, and stares out the sunny window, and has the feeling that he would rather be anywhere in the world than in this cottage. *I should have just stayed in Beirut. Or London,* he thinks. *At least they have a fucking Labour Party in London.* He stares out the window some more, then at the dark TV screen, then at a newspaper lying on the floor.

He contemplates the idea of going into the bedroom to see Irene. He knows that she is probably lying on the bed, probably trying to read, but unable to concentrate. He knows her so well. His body tells him to go and lay everything to rest. Once and for all. But something stops him. His chest tightens. And something stops him.

Instead, he picks up a pen from the floor and scribbles some lines onto the back of an envelope:

> *Why do you make banana bread*
> *When I ask you for love?*
> *Why do you stare at me blankly*
> *When I ask for your soul?*
> *Why do I find shadow*
> *In the heart of every light?*
> *Why have I become chained*
> *in the land of the free?*

Laying down the pen, he closes his eyes. Afternoon comes. And evening. Shadows fall again as the day ends the same way it started. Momentous emptiness stretches out before both of them. The earth between them has become a minefield where nothing can grow.

11
Home Front

P.M.
A man and a woman are alone in their cottage in a foggy alley of town.

Nightfall
In a darkened barroom, a poet walks onto a makeshift stage.

It was night
A man and a woman sit side by side on a couch in their tiny living room. They're watching a made-for-television movie.
They sit on opposite sides of the couch.

First blue, then purple, then the black of night
The poet takes the microphone and looks out at the room veiled in a haze of smoke. The bar is full of urbanites, passersby who just happen to be there, and a regular drunk or two, slumping in the shadowy corners.
The poet takes a deep breath and closes her eyes. She pauses and lets out a long sigh.

Night of a door opening. No stars, no moon. It was night in the city of collapsing dreams
The barroom is alive with the sound of conversations,

exchanges of money, bursts of laughter. There's a TV playing above the bar with the sound on high, flashing make believe colors into the dim room.

Cry all night if you want to, the poet whispers into the microphone tentatively. Almost no one in the bar looks up.

It was a night like any other

The man and woman are slumped down on their couch, watching a melodrama about a woman whose child has been abducted by her estranged husband. The woman embarks on her own personal search for the child. She quits her job. She becomes obsessed, loses friends.

The man and the woman, on opposite sides of the couch, haven't spoken to each other all day.

Night of a door closing

Cry all night if you want to, the poet says again. Her voice is intense, full of blues. A few of the talkers in the bar join the listeners. The bartender clicks the mute button on the TV and moves down the bar, closer to the stage; the noise in the room drops down to the voice of one:

Cry all night if you want to. The system can't hear, the poet speaks to the crowd, her long dreadlocks falling into her face.

She starts to rock back and forth, shaking her head, adding rhythm to her words.

It was a California night

The man and the woman continue to watch the predictable downhill spiral. The lone woman whose child has been kidnapped hires a shady private detective. He's a recovering alcoholic, hasn't held a job in years. Grumpy, slovenly, he is touched by her desperation and takes the case.

The man in the cottage goes to get a bottle of beer from the fridge. It's his fourth beer that night. The woman says nothing. They haven't spoken in two days. She sits on the couch and listens to the sound of a siren not too far in the distance.

No moon, no stars. No point of reference.

The whole barroom is listening. The poet is louder now, trembling. Her eyes are still closed as she speaks her words, each one bitten off and bitter:

> *Beat your head and collapse*
> *'til your shadow kisses the floor—*
> *The system can't see.*

> *Scream and wail through it all*
> *Beg for pardon, a deal...*
> *The system has no mind, no soul*
> *No, no.*

She says this last line almost Reggae, almost singing, *No, no.* She shakes her head with every beat.

You say to yourself, *Let it pass quickly*. The traffic sounds like waves, waves like memory, memory—like broken glass. In this night, the poet wields each syllable like a knife.

She commands the stage fiercely now. No one's ever seen a poet like this in here before.

> *The system has no mind, no soul,*
> *just the mouth of a soldier*
> *who's trained to behave*
> *like a wall.*

It was a night of no beginning and no end, where anything that can happen has happened. And will happen again.
The man comes back from the kitchen with a fresh bottle of beer. They continue watching the movie about the abducted child. The child actress is the classic Hollywood tomboy— precocious, self-assured, making wisecracks as her weirdo father drives her away on his lunatic roadtrip, destination unknown.

Just turn it off, the woman says with an edge in her voice. He doesn't answer, so they both keep watching, unable to pull away from what they've already started.

It was night on a part of the earth that was taking a turn for the worse. An orange haze hangs over the City, swollen from streetlights and cars and reckless neon signs flashing.
On the TV, the private detective and the distraught mother are slowly but surely falling in love. Although they haven't located the girl yet, his work with her has been redemptive. He feels "alive again." Little by little he has been transformed—he begins taking care of his appearance—he shaves, tucks in his shirt, loses weight. *Mary Ellen*, he says to her at his front door, *Don't go yet. Stay.* All of a sudden the screen goes black. The man has flicked it off with a quick finger. The room goes black.

> *Cry all night your exile, your loneliness.*
> *Your rage*
>
> *If you have the will to remember*
> *Your ancestor's passage*
> *across oceans of dark secrets.*

It is quiet in the room for an instant then the man says angrily, *I can't believe I came from the most beautiful land in the*

147

world...to wind up in this...military base.... The man is standing near the window that looks out on the alley. The sound of a siren catches fire in his ears. He takes another large sip of the beer and turns around to face her.

What do you want me to say? the woman asks. *I don't even know why you're so angry at me. You act as though everything that's wrong with the world is my fault.*

No, I act like everything that's wrong with the world is wrong with you too!

Why? Why do you say that?

You know.

It was night not far from the sea. It was a night on the edge of a continent that was said to be slowly falling into the sea.

The poet says:

> *Cry all night*
> *Cause you can't remember*
>
> *how it felt to be whole.*
>
> *and you never know*
> *after dark*
>
> *where the flying bird goes*

What the hell are you talking about? the woman says angrily. *You are so full of it.*

No, he raises his voice, *you are. You don't care about anything except your own personal happiness. There is a massacre going on in Iraq and you want to make banana bread and watch movies?*

Ahh! I can't believe you! she screeches. *I'm the one who said we should turn off the stupid TV....What do you want me to do about the war?*

This is not a war. This is a massacre. Desert Storm?

Where did they get that metaphor? This is not a storm.
People, children are dying. But that means nothing to you.

The woman is in tears all of a sudden. She is remembering everything that has happened between them. Intimacies and desire, the smell of eucalyptus on sunset walks in the park, soft blossoms falling on them in springtime as they lay body to body in the long green grass. His poetry in her ears as they made love in the attic they shared that first summer together. Where did all these sweet moments go?

But his voice is relentless: *This war means nothing to you because nothing means anything to you people anymore. Don't you know, can't you see that this is really happening?*

Of course I can. Her tears are still falling.

Are you sure about that? he asks. But she remains speechless. She knows anything that she might say would come out completely wrong.

There's a poet on a stage in a bar. Her face is brown, her brow—downbeat. She makes eye contact only with the floor. Her lips crowd the microphone, so even at a whisper she's heard.

> *Cry all night*
> *'til you mark with tears*
> *the perimeter of your grief.*
>
> *Cry all night*
> *'til your eyes are too blind to see*
>
> *But just don't*
> *become part*
>
> *of this cold-blooded world.*
> *Don't sell your heart,*
>
> *your truth, your soul.*

The poet says these lines with slow emphasis and with a sad nodding smile that creaks out between squinted eyes. She says the word "soul" with soul, drawing out the "o" in a way that lets you know she believes there is such a thing, such a necessary thing as soul.

There's a woman trapped in the shadows beneath a man she doesn't know anymore. He stands above her saying, *What you need is to find someone more like you. I'm getting out of here.*

I'm getting out of here, he screams again, throwing his bottle across the room. It crashes against the wall. *I'm getting out. Out!* He rushes out the door and slams it behind him.

There is silence. The poet has finished her performance. The muted television hanging from the ceiling flashes its predictable images above the room. A little white house on a quiet tree-lined street. A man, woman, and child hugging and grinning at each other on the stairs in front of the door. Even with the sound off, anyone could interpret the closing scenes from a bad TV movie that no one's been watching.

The poet breaks the silence saying: *I would like to dedicate that last poem to the innocent people who are being killed right now.* The poet stops and looks out at the people in the bar.

It was night in a city near the sea, a city that was said to be slowly falling into the sea. Somewhere in the city a child cries out for her mother. But the mother is nowhere to be seen.

There will be no question-and-answer period tonight. As soon as the poet finishes her speech she walks off the stage and disappears out the door and onto the Boulevard. And no one hears from her again.

Soon, the bored bartender flips on the sound. The movie that no one has been watching has just ended.

Now the credits roll down the screen, unnoticed
like a wounded dove, like a message in a bottle, blowing across twelve thousand miles of stormy seas.

12
A Visit to the Dead

Oblivion is the only cure for agony
—Kathy Acker

A girl child has fallen from a high window in slow motion. She was last standing on some kind of edge, a building or bridge, but now she's falling. She screams for help—in slow motion—a look of terror on her face. But it's too late. Dropping into space, spread-eagle, she screams "heeeelp," then lands with a crash.

Across desert red landscapes Irene is driving.

Past desert red rocks Irene is driving. She sleeps and wakes, falls asleep then wakes with the image of the falling child in her mind. She says:

Dream, you can't destroy me. It's the middle of the night, near midnight, but not exactly; and she is still driving across the desert of No. She starts the car again and pulls onto the road. At sixty miles an hour, she finally heaves a deep sigh.

Rushing onward, she opens the window and hears and feels the whistling of warm sweet air. She wags a hand outside, dragging her fingers in the wind. One tear streaks her cheek, but she does not wipe it. She lets it dry in place and continues on the unlit highway.

She's on her way to visit her friend who is dying in a city

on the other side of the desert. To see her friend who is dying of breast cancer. The disease has metastasized to all parts of the body. Erratic growths, lumps, malignant cells and tumors have been found in the far nooks and crannies of her flesh. She is due to die any day now in an alternative hospice, smoking marijuana with Buddhist monks. Any day now Kathy will be dead, and so Irene is racing with time across the desert.

She is heading due east, but knows that her destination is more west than the West Coast. She's been to that town before. She knows that it's a town of bulging belt buckles and ten-gallon hats. Cowboys adorned in turquoise and leather have grown so backwards into history that they consider *themselves* indigenous. These men work with Tandy leather kits, tooling Navajo designs into belts, weaving dream catchers far into the night. But on the outskirts of town is where she'll find Kathy, in the foothills.

Irene remembers the first time she met Kathy. So long ago. She was still living in that beach house, a place filled with bad feelings. The best thing that had ever happened to her was the day she met Kathy. She was taking a bus downtown, riding alone on a clear sunny morning. There were three men on the bus next to her, giving her a hard time. Stuff like:

Come on, baby, give us some money.

Come on, honey, come sit on my lap.

Come on, sexy, turn around and talk to us.

Irene was too embarrassed to tell them to mind their own business, so instead she sat mortified, looking out the window, trying to ignore them. Meanwhile they kept up the talk, *So you think you're too good for us? Don't want to even look at us?* She was just about to turn around and tell them to back off when all of the sudden down the aisle walked Kathy. Her hair was bleached and shorn, razor short. She was tattooed up and down her arms, wearing red lipstick. She stood like a proud post-modern goddess in the midst of them.

The bus lunged forward but she remained standing like a hero in the midst of the rabble. Queen Clytemnestra—not only willing but *able* to kill a husband for the sake of a daughter. She didn't have to say a word; the men were cast into a state of speechless apprehension. From the looks of her, she definitely had a switchblade tucked away in a boot.

Next stop, the men descended, shoving each other down the stairwell of the bus. Kathy sat down immediately next to Irene and started talking in a nonstop monologue.

I'm a morning person, really. I simply love the fresh air. Makes my blood circulate. The few people who have read my books probably assume I'm a night person, but no. There's also this idea that I want to kill people. But actually I'm a pacifist. I got into meditation in the 70s. Kathy started knocking wildly on the window, waving to a man on the street. As soon as he waved back she continued talking, *Critics assume that I am basically one and the same as my narrators who are often violent, sociopathic. Typical idiotic mistake. Do I want to smash the system? Obviously. But guess where I am heading right now? To this great little Chinese laundry in town to pick up my favorite leather jacket.... Great people—the Asians—I admire their history and culture.*

Kathy reached into her black fanny pack and took out a small pink case saying, *always carry my pills with me...y'never know when I might not go home at night...* She ranged her fingers down the line of little orange pills and popped the last one out of the foil and into her mouth, continuing, *What was that T.S. Eliot line? "I have measured out my life in coffee spoons." Now we have a new measure for our days, it's called birth control... The Pill is just another leash we're on. Someone should write about the link between monthly bleeding of women, Visa/Master card accounts...the co-optation of the lunar schedule.... You see what I'm driving at.*

Irene was listening to Kathy and nodding her head, adding *Uh-Huh's,* and *Yes's,* and *I know's* to Kathy's speech.

By the time the bus reached the park where she was planning to attend an outdoor concert, she turned and invited Kathy for coffee. She replied, *I don't drink coffee anymore, but I know a great place to have Indian Chai....*

After that day, Irene and Kathy became friends. Kathy urged Irene to study harder and introduced her to currents of thought that might be useful to her. She was a mentor to her, and her words were always with her, *You've always allowed men, the system, to use you. It's time to fight back!*

All of that was long ago. Before Khalid. Before the mess that was made of everything between them. Before the war.

Now Irene is alone, trying to see Kathy one more time before she dies. She travels through desert landscapes, past the red hills and rock formations. And she wonders what's in them to make them so red. *It must be blood. Apache blood. It's the pierced heart of the Great Spirit who is wounded, but not yet gone.*

Why does the earth make us and then take us away? Why does the world bring us great joy and love, then snatch it away so violently? Why does every road seem to end at a fence or a parking lot in front of a red brick hospital? The world needs you, Kathy. You are the only honest artist. Why do you have to go like this, with your whole body falling apart?

She remembers again how in the old days she used to show up late at Kathy's place after a fight with Khalid. *You never asked questions,* she spoke in her mind to Kathy. *You'd just let me in and we'd stay up all night smoking and drinking and listening to grainy recordings of underground poets. Or we would read from your books. Then sometimes you'd say, "Let's call him." And we'd call Khalid in the middle of the night and invite him over. And then the three of us would stay up 'til dawn talking and laughing.*

Khalid used to tell Irene: *Kathy's the only free woman I know, including you.*

And Irene would say, *No one's free, including you. Everyone lives within the boundaries of their own minds and bodies and history.*

But if Kathy happened to be there she'd say something like, *Wrong, Irene. You have to* learn *to cross the boundaries of this bourgeois identity thing. The whole "individual" thing is a fiction, it's a story they keep shoving down our throats. It goes back to Rimbaud, actually earlier, to the mystics. Don't ever forget this: There is no "I."*

To Khalid, Kathy would say: *You idiot! You've got this marvelous woman in your life. What I would do for a woman like Irene! For fucksake, get your act together!* Whenever Kathy would make one of these pronouncements, Khalid would become uncharacteristically sheepish.

Now Kathy's flesh is being destroyed minute by minute. It's the fast kind of cancer, the one that is unstoppable. Her control genes are on the fritz and the wrong cells are splitting and multiplying, not slowing for anything. Both breasts gone, she blames it on her mother and her mother's mother down the line. *This is what I've been given, see? Disease! It's the fatal dose of what I've already been living with,* Kathy said on the phone, *but...I can handle it.* Irene has heard through friends that Kathy's bones protrude through the skin and they crumble if she gets out of bed.

Far into the night, with radio playing crackly country tunes, Irene stays frozen behind the wheel. Eyes glued to the road, mind glued to the road, she pushes it as fast as she can. Speeds along, blinks along, with nothing to do but think and remember. Phrases flash in her brain like: *Bats in the belfry, Love is just a four letter word,* and other bits of language that make no sense like *"your fat emptiness," "a covey of secret wishes," "spasmodic."* And she repeats mantras to herself like, *I am nothing. Let the breeze of life blow through me,* but in the solitary confinement of the vehicle nothing blows. And

when she begins to sing a song to herself, her voice comes
out sounding arid and cracked:

> *Ne me quitte pas*
> *Il faut oublier*
> *Tout peut s'oublier*
> *Qui s'enfuit déjà...*

She sings this song the way Nina Simone sings it—in a
sad gasping voice with an awkward French accent. And she
sings it knowing, as Nina did, what the words mean. *Don't
leave me. We must forget. Everything can be forgotten which
is already passing. We can forget the misunderstandings, the
lost time. Don't leave me.*

Irene's eyes begin to cross and see double, closing of
their own accord. She pulls down the frontage road and parks
the car. Releasing the small plastic lever next to her, she
pushes the driver's scat to a completely flat position. With
her arms folded behind her head, she nods off and dreams
immediately

*that she is with Khalid, walking up and down a hilly ridge
next to the Pacific Ocean. The path goes up and down, up
and down; and the two of them are walking quietly. The
feeling is one of peace. There's some grass growing and
blowing in the wind and they continue walking with no
destination. She feels so happy just to be there with him. He
says to her in Arabic: "Al Shams bidha itnam." The sun is
going to sleep. And then suddenly the sun is setting. And she
says to him in Arabic: "Ya Hiati," my love, my life. She reaches
out and looks into his black eyes that flash like lightning.
They are standing on the edge of a field of tall swaying grass.
She notices that the land is filled with gopher holes. Far
below—the blue sea crashes rhythmically against rocks and
cliff. She leans over to kiss him and he turns his face and
says to her, "Jump. Why don't you just jump and get it over
with."*

Irene is driving across a desert.

It's the desert of love. It's the desert where everything that *can* happen *has* happened. It's the desert of no future, no gods, no reason. It is an imaginary desert, a desert of the imaginary that has stretched its dominion into the real world.

She is driving in a wasteland where all she hears is her own voice. This is her landscape. Her friend is dying. There are dry riverbeds and hills and roads and each has a name. It's a desert with many names, but the ancient ones are all but forgotten, replaced with state parks where nature-loving people go rock climbing and camping with the latest nylon gear. Irene passed two of them a few hours ago. When she stopped for gas, a tanned young man standing near his 4-wheel-drive vehicle was telling his friend, "   ." And the other guy put his big hiking boot up on the bumper and responded, "   ."

All is dark and abandoned. Irene wakes up and raises the seat and turns on the car and drives some more. After several miles she turns off at a rest area. It's the quiet kind: no restaurant/gift shop, no gas or other commodities, just the plain bathrooms and a small kiosk featuring free maps and brochures. Irene gets out of the car. It's almost morning. She stands up and stretches her arms in the warm breeze and then walks to the phone. Slipping a load of change into the slot, she dials the number written on a rumpled envelope. A weary voice answers, *Hello.*

I know it's too early to call. I just wanted to tell you I'm on my way.

The voice says, *You didn't wake me. I can't sleep anymore.*

How do you feel?

My own cells don't recognize me. This is the Dionysian agony I've been talking about all along.

Are they giving you anything to help?

I'm on drugs. It reminds me I'm not real anyway.

You're real to me, Irene says.

And the voice says, *No, as of now, I've become a character in someone's little novel.*

Irene pauses for a second then says, *Do we like this writer? Who is it? Marquis de Sade?*

Kathy laughs weakly, then says, *I have to go.*

Irene hears the click at the other end of the line and stands there for a minute holding the phone, looking at the sky. There's a thin band of red on the eastern horizon which gradually widens. She watches this streak of light, then the glow of sun—minutes before it emerges from the horizon.

She hangs up the phone and walks toward the car; the little tourism stand catches her eye. In the violet light she finds herself staring absently at the rack of pamphlets. One glossy brochure stands out. It announces in bold letters: *Visit Indian Burial Caves!* There's a picture of a happy white family peering into a deep dark cavern. Under the picture in smaller letters it reads: *Experience the Mystery of Ancient Death Rituals! Actual Indian Artifacts! Guided Tours Daily. Gift/Book Shop open daily 10am-6pm.* Irene studies the brochure and for a split second actually considers paying a visit to the site. For an instant she imagines that she will go to these caves and start chanting or screaming, *I won't buy a ticket to visit the dead! I won't buy a ticket to visit the dead!* But the image ends there—she turns around and walks to the car. There will be no visit.

In ten minutes Irene will pass the first billboard for the burial attraction. In twenty minutes she'll pass the last. She drives as fast as she can, but she does not arrive in time. She will never see Kathy's visitors milling in the shade of fruit trees in the courtyard, whispering in Spanglish. She won't see the nurses and the curanderas preparing herbal washes and burning sage, saying that Kathy is no longer in pain. That she has reached the stage where tragedy and ecstasy meet; that her spirit is re-merging with the numinous.

When Irene walks to the front desk and asks for Kathy's room, the young Mexican woman pauses and looks up into Irene's eyes. *I'm sorry,* she says, looking concerned. Irene searches the young woman's brown eyes for the meaning of her words. Searches briefly, then knows. *Lo siento,* the young receptionist says again. Irene's heart sinks and she begins to panic. *Come with me,* the girl says gently and guides Irene towards a cheerful looking sitting room with tropical plants and a window with a view.

No, no, Irene says, *I want to see Kathy. I want to say goodbye.* The receptionist nods and takes Irene out through a courtyard filled with sunlight and trees and a few people in wheelchairs. Then they enter a cool dark corridor that leads to another corridor. The young woman opens the door to a cold room with nothing in it but a huge metal freezer. She opens the middle drawer and rolls out a medium-sized mound. Slowly, she unzips the bag; her bright red manicured fingernails glow against the drab canvas.

After pushing the flaps aside, the girl walks out of the room leaving Irene and Kathy alone together. Irene can now see that it really is Kathy in there, thin and white and cold. Her bleached crop of hair is in place. She still has the trace of a smile on her tiny face. As if she had told one final joke to a friend before passing.

Kathy, Irene says, placing her forehead on her friend's frozen arm. The frost from the freezer is tumbling out of the drawer like mist over Niagara Falls. Pouring across the two of them.

Kathy, she says. *Where did you go?*

With her head on Kathy's arm, Irene waits for Kathy to say something. But nothing comes. Just the hum of the big silver freezer as the motor turns on. The whir of the machine is the only noise in the room.

You were the one who was always crossing boundaries, Irene says with her head still down on Kathy's arm. *You were the real.* She lifts her head and then cradles Kathy's face in her hands saying, *I'm gonna miss you. I'm not gonna let you down.*

The hand of death has brushed ice across Kathy's brow. The hand of death has turned flesh to ice, has turned thoughts to silence, has turned a vibrant mind to dust and stone. Has allowed a human being to be placed in a canvas bag, zipped up, and placed in cold storage.

The hand of death can take a person, can take a friend, can swindle you of your every last plan. The hand of death can steal the consolation of companionship, can plunder the child and then childhood itself. But it cannot steal words that have already been spoken.

Even as Irene finally leaves the room, walks down the hospice corridors, drives alone back through the very same night through which she has just come, as she continues on with her life, nothing will be able to erase Kathy's prose:

The ceiling of languages is falling down. Either add to this rubble or shove at least some of it away.

The streets were now the property of cars. The cars were now the property of those who had real jobs. The men who worked in the corporations or driving to and from the corporations inside mirrored Styrofoam cars, they were no longer visible. They were dead. I was confused to the point of psychosis because I wasn't sure what I was.

What is language? Does anyone speak to anyone? Is language computer language, journalese, dictation of expectation and behavior, announcement of the allowed possibilities or reality? Does language control like money?

My agenda? I don't have an agenda and I'm not sure who I am! Who am I? Women are only allowed in society if they become substitute men.

Wha? What? Juliet's dead. Well that's no reason to wake me up in the middle of the night. She deserved to die, since she wasn't worth anything, especially economically....

These are the rules: Exaggerate pain because the

government wants to ignore what I feel.... This society that worships money or the lack of values has petrified and immortalized all our monstrosities.

Why do I have so many feelings?
Where are the toilet arrangements?
So you're gonna die, dope?
No, I'm already dead.

13
The Sinking Island

It's nighttime in a city that is said to be slowly falling into the sea. A city of ribbons tied to mailboxes and condominium security gates. Half-hidden in eastbound fog, it's a city of small-time provincial dreams, and a big-time bayside conference center.

I'm getting out of here, hangs in Khalid's head, *I'm getting out of here,* shoots through his head. Not like rain or hunger or thunder, but like the hiss of spray paint on a crumbling wall.

Khalid is walking—out of the courtyard of cottages where he lives with Irene. He is leaving her. It's impossible between them. They've been through too much. He knows he still loves her, and yet…and yet…they are too different.

What do game shows have in common with uprisings, disco with debke? Shopping malls with olive trees? What do they—he and Irene, have in common besides illusions, and a few memories? He feels that they will never be able to understand each other. They are from two separate worlds. Two worlds at odds with each other.

Desire and pain surge below the surface of his dark skin, visible only in the taut grimace of his lips.

I'm in hell, also hangs in his head, in English, not in Arabic.

In Arabic he would tend to say the opposite: *Ana mit awid. I'm used to it by now.*

Khalid is walking. He storms out the door of his house and then out the front gate toward the Boulevard. At the corner he finds himself face to face with a ballooning blue and yellow Blockbuster video store. There are posters hanging in the glass window that advertise movies like "Not Without My Daughter" and "Delta Force," and in them he sees his reflection—blurred and distorted by the colors of the night.

This is Khalid's eternal landscape—the real world—a world that has lost its innocence and grace. To him, "getting real" doesn't mean what it means to most men at 30—a regular job, car payments, establishing a permanent site of safe sex. "Getting real" means maintaining an attitude of deep suspicion. He's a reader of signs and gestures and has come to terms with the fact that humans, for the most part, are a race of incorrigible liars. And whenever he walks—even when he's thinking, or dreaming, or talking—he is always acutely conscious of the precise distance between wherever he might be going and every other place he's been.

And the one place that is always on his mind is Beirut.

Beirut is the language and the voice of loss. Beirut is the shattered song playing in his senses. A song of endless destruction. In an instant Khalid hears the opening bars and then the whole melody is resuscitated with its unbearable refrain, the refrain that carries a single tune, the tune called farewell.

In this night of lonely walking in the land of loneliness, Khalid hears the voice of Beirut coming back again. He hears his own cousin Christine's voice.

Where are you going? she asks him. Her voice splits the night and it's so real in his ear that he prepares to give her an answer: *I'm just going out, Christine.* But he silences himself. Instead he allows her to keep speaking and hears the rest of the story. Instead he allows himself to travel down the length of his memory to a place and a time that are lost forever.

Where are you going? Christine asked Sayeed as he was heading out the front door. She placed her hand on his arm lightly and looked him in the eye. *When are you going to stop hanging around with those twins?*

It was early spring in 1975 and Khalid was in the ninth grade, living as a member of the Aseelah family for almost a full year. He was going to school in the day and working at the family clothing store in the afternoons. He spent as much free time as he could with Bilal and Naseem, although they were forbidden to enter the house.

When are you going to stop? Christine repeated again, firmly, with a note of concern. She thought that it was in his own best interest to make friends with the clean-cut young men at his private school. Sayeed had nothing to say for himself. But he looked over at Lydia, his other cousin, who was sitting at the table reading her newspaper. She looked up at Christine and said, *what you MEAN to say is: When is he going to stop hanging around those Muslims, right?*

No, Christine said, *what I mean to say is that they are not kids anymore. The best those twins can hope for is to become fedayeen. And that's natural for people of their ilk. But Sayeed is gifted. He has a future.*

A future? Lydia smirked, *in Tel Zaatar? When are you going to open your eyes? Those brothers are willing to die for their homeland while you are busy brushing up on your French.* While the two sisters argued, Sayeed quietly slipped out the door. He knew he had Lydia on his side. She would make his point for him. Soon he'd be walking side by side with his friends, snacking on a shawarma sandwich and talking politics.

Naseem and Bilal's father worked as an office clerk for the PLO in the Tel Zaatar refugee camp, so they often met at their father's building which was only a few minutes from the house on the edge of the camp. The two brothers had now become fierce defenders of the Fatah faction. They were always trying to convince Sayeed that they should all three join the movement together. The discussion was ongoing and continuous, like a slow dripping faucet, no matter what they were doing—window shopping down Hamra, or visiting friends, or sitting down by the beach flirting with every passing girl.

Under Lydia's influence, Sayeed leaned further towards the left. Lydia was an ardent feminist who had resisted marriage on principle. She was politically active, and read Al-Hadaf, a socialist newspaper, on a regular basis. Sayeed couldn't help but agree with his smart, impassioned cousin. Sometimes he caught himself quoting her very words. *You can't have a successful struggle for Palestine without a socialist revolution in the Arab world.* From Lydia's library, Sayeed had already begun reading the works of Marx, Engels, and Lenin. Their reflections on mankind's *resolvable* alienation had entered his bloodstream like cool refreshing water.

As soon as Sayeed slipped out of the house that evening, Sitti Mary got in on the family squabble, and so did Christine's husband Moussa, who was usually quiet. *Lydia,* Moussa started, *you don't seem to realize how precarious our situation is right now. Don't you know that the whole thing is about to explode? Then where will you be? With your committees and your revolution!* Moussa was referring to the fact, which he found extremely unpleasant, that Lydia was an active member of several Palestinian women's committees, organizing the camps, fund-raising for various improvement campaigns, circulating newsletters and flyers.

In these regular disputes, Sitti Mary tended to side with Lydia, having the most bitter memories of hunger and hardship. *Finally,* she said, *we are trying to unite. We are not waiting anymore for Nasser, for the kings, for the Arabs.*

Just let me tell you what my customers say, Moussa responded dryly. *They tell me this: You Palestinians are destroying Lebanon.*

Not ALL Lebanese think that way, Lydia jumped in. *Your customers are hardly representative!*

Within weeks of this family argument, the civil war in Lebanon would erupt. And from the very outset, with its street fighting, revenge killings, and religious divisions, it was clear that it would be a gruesome conflict. A tidal wave of blood and retribution would wash up onto Beirut's shores and leave only ruins and bitterness behind it. But there in the room that evening, they didn't foresee what was coming. They would speculate, argue, and disagree about everything, but nothing could stop what was coming.

The sun had finally set and the room was filling with deep shadows. By now Sayeed was long gone, walking towards his meeting place with Bilal and Naseem. Lydia was about to stand up and storm out of the room. Just then, Christine reached over to switch on the wall lamp. The room was suddenly filled with light.

Allah y'nawar allaiki, Lydia said out of habit. It was a traditional blessing that slipped from Lydia's lips. Lydia smiled at the double meaning of this phrase she had used and then repeated it again: *May God grant you light!* Christine smiled too and walked over and placed her hand on her sister's arm, repeating the phrase, *May God grant YOU light*!

You know, we Arabs say nice things to each other, Khalid once told Irene in their early months together. *Our language is full of blessings. We have a blessing and a wish for every occasion you can imagine.*

Are you homesick? Irene asked.

Homesick? Khalid repeated. It was a term that he usually associated with nostalgic college students away from their parents for the first time. Now when she put this question to him, it finally made sense. *Yes,* he said, *I don't have a home. And it makes me sick.* Then he added, *but I have my places. Places that belong to me, places that know me.*

What about here? she asked him.

I once was very excited to be in the U.S., he told her. *I went through a long phase of loving this country. I read the classic American authors, Hemingway, Steinbeck, Walt Whitman. I saw the great old movies. Soaked up the music. Did you know that for two years I had an American flag on my car?*

What happened? Irene interrupted.

I found out that America didn't want to know me back.

It was morning and they were preparing breakfast. Khalid was loading the table with little plates of olives, tomato and cucumber slices, hummus, flat bread, olive oil, and zaatar, a tart mixture of thyme, lemon, sumac, sesame seeds, and salt.

Zee breakfast is served, he proclaimed in a silly French accent à la Brando in *The Last Tango.* There was always an artistic dimension to whatever he did. He swirled a spoon in the hummus, making an impromptu design on its surface.

The two sat down to eat the feast. Both of them *mmmmed* and *yummmed* over all the goodies covering the table. Khalid dipped a warm piece of bread into the olive oil, then into the zaatar. *Taste this, my love,* he said.

I've had it before, Khalid, Irene protested.

It's more delicious from your lover's hand, he said and held it to her lips. *This is thyme from the Holy Land, prepared by Aunt Salwa.* She opened her mouth and took the bite and agreed that it *was* more delicious from his hand.

When Jesus said "Man does not live on bread alone," do you know what he meant by that? Khalid asked.

What did he mean?

He meant that you have to have bread with olive oil and zaatar, of course!

167

April 1975 was the official outbreak of the war in Lebanon. In the first months, the street fighting didn't affect Sayeed and the Aseelah family directly, except in the way it divided them even more. Lydia told Sayeed that the conservatives wanted to get rid of "the Palestinian problem" by any means, including murderous rampages.

Christine meanwhile believed that the refugees had been ungrateful for the hospitality of the Lebanese people.

What hospitality? Lydia would say. *Do you call these camps hospitality? And besides, we didn't ASK to be here!* These conversations would go on and on, night after night, exacerbated by the terrifying news of massacres, kidnappings, and roadblocks where people could be killed for simply having the wrong religion or nationality.

During Lydia and Christine's disagreements, their mother would just wring her hands, crying, *If we were only at home in Safad, we'd be fine.* Every time she said these words, she pictured her own home in those green hills.

There was a cobalt blue bowl that used to sit in the stone windowsill of her old home. Her husband, Aisa, had bought it from the Armenians in Jerusalem on one of his trips. Sometimes she put figs in it from the tree in the courtyard— to let them ripen. Mary wept whenever she remembered that bowl. In it she saw an entire previous life spread before her eyes.

We didn't kill the Jews in Germany, she'd weep, *so why did they have to come and take our country?*

As the fighting in Beirut grew more fierce, Sayeed stopped going to school, which was in a Christian neighborhood. His classmates had begun to bully and harass him, although he too was from a Christian family. For a while he continued to go to work everyday at the store. But then one night the family shop was hit by a shell. And so they closed down the store too. Within a year, all semblance of normal life had been stripped away, and the ugly truth was laid bare: The city had descended into an inferno.

Why would anyone want to live in the Middle East? This was a question that Khalid had been asked many times during the eight years that he had been in the United States. Or this: *I can't understand why there's so much fighting in the Middle East.* Or: *Don't you just feel blessed to be in this country?*

Khalid would answer this type of question according to his mood. One of his answers was: *If all the world ever saw of the United States were the murder rates and urban riots, then no one would think much of America either!*

Or he might say: *The Israelites, the Greeks, the Romans, the Crusaders, the Turks, then the British, French, and then the European Zionists didn't seem to think that it was such a worthless place to invade, did they?*

Each time someone asked him this type of question, it was a renewed source of vexation for Khalid. He was irked that many people just didn't seem to grasp the most fundamental premise, the basic concept that people in other countries are normal human beings. Living, breathing, eating, loving people who come from rich cultures and ancient civilizations. With children, beliefs, music, dreams, and conflicts of their own.

We're people! Khalid mutters out loud as he walks east on the Boulevard away from home. *We're not just newspaper pictures. We're people*, he shouts louder. *People!* But it's nighttime. The streets are deserted and he feels even lonelier to know that everyone else is at home watching a new television show called "Desert Storm" on CNN. The public space is abandoned, so Khalid is alone with his thoughts and ravings and whatever else he carries inside.

To this day, Khalid can still see their faces clearly. His first true friends in this world. Bilal and Naseem. How clearly he can see them in life. Bilal's unrestrained crop of kinky hair. His dark face always filled with a combination of anxiety and laughter. Naseem's tilted smile, his tall frame, jittery with perpetual motion. How clearly Khalid can see the two of them leaning like men on the concrete walls of Shatila, popping sunflower seeds into their mouths one by one. He sees them in their 1970s clothing—bell-bottom hip huggers and longish hair and printed shirts. That's how he'll see them forever.

He can still hear Naseem playing his oud in the afternoons in Tel Zaatar. Naseem sang all the traditional folksongs and had started to make up his own sad little ballads. *Oh woe! Oh woe upon these times,* he sang, *where blood fills the streets like rain. And love is a forgotten tune. Where, oh, where is the innocence of youth?*

Under Christine's orders, Bilal and Naseem were barred from entering the Aseelah household. So instead of knocking on the door of the house, they often called out to Sayeed in loud voices and he came running down to join them.

Just down the alley from the house there was a low cement wall around an empty lot. The three of them used to go and sit there and talk and smoke Marlboros. Sometimes when a little kid came wandering down the alley, they would call out to him to bring some cola or coffee or tea from a nearby café. And the scruffy, bedraggled child would hold out his hand for some money. In minutes the kid would be back with a tray of tea and glasses. Plus a small amount of change that the older boys would let him keep.

Once during the first year of the war, right after the Aseelah business was shelled, they were sitting on that wall and Naseem was saying, *You know, Sayeed, it's about time we rename you.* Naseem announced this as if he and Bilal had been discussing the issue for months.

Bilal immediately jumped in and confirmed Naseem's statement. *Yeah, Sayeed, you need a new name. We can't just keep calling you "the happy one."*

What are you talking about? Sayeed looked back and forth between his two friends who had conspiratorial looks on their faces.

Well, everyone in the struggle gets a new name. Like how Arafat is Abu Ammar. And don't forget Abu Jihad and the rest.

With everything that's happening nowadays, you just can't go around being "happy" anymore.

Right, said Sayeed going along with his friends' teasing, *You guys just tell me what to change my name to, and I will.*

Since you're mostly into your books and poetry, we should call you something literary. How about Abu Kitab, father of books or Abu Fikr, father of ideas.

Then there was silence while the three of them brainstormed possible new names for Sayeed. *Abu Zikra, the father of Memory,* Naseem threw in.

Y'know it doesn't have to be father of anything, said Sayeed. *Why don't you just come up with a nice poetic name. If you come up with something good, I'll use it.*

At that moment the sound of automatic gunfire ripped through the air and several shells exploded in quick succession. They estimated that it was probably right along the line that separated East and West Beirut, a few kilometers away.

These sounds had become so familiar that they could be easily ignored—as long as they seemed far enough away. And yet they were gloomy and full of foreboding, these anonymous echoes. One day they'd hear the sounds of an explosion and think nothing of it, the next day they'd read in the newspaper that an apartment building had been demolished. With six small children burned inside.

As the bombardments echoed on, followed by machine-gun fire tattering the air, there was a lull in the boys' friendly chatter. Each, for a moment, abandoned the conversation for an excursion into his own private thoughts. Sayeed was thinking about Aunt Salwa back in his village. He recalled her soft face and loving eyes, and remembered their days together in the bakery when he was a small boy. He missed her bread, the smells of the bakery, the stories she'd tell under the grapevines behind the house on summer evenings. He often wondered if she would be willing to leave Palestine to join them in Beirut. Then he scoffed at his own absurd thought, *In the middle of this? What an idea!* He sighed out loud.

What, asked Bilal?

Nothing, said Sayeed. *Nothing, just thinking crazy thoughts. But listen, Naseem and Bilal. When all of this fighting is over…what do you want to do with your lives?*

His friends looked at each other, stumped, as if they had never given it a moment's reflection. Finally Naseem spoke up in tone of bravado, *I already know what I'm gonna be. I'm going to be an airline pilot. I'll get to wear one of those nice clean uniforms, and fly all over the world. I'll fly to Europe and meet all of those good looking French girls.*

Yes, and I'll be the guy bringing drinks to all the passengers, added Bilal, picking up the cheap plastic tray that was sitting on the wall next to them. He jumped down from the wall and bowed with the tray in front of the others, *Excusez-moi, monsieur, would you like some tea?* They all started laughing.

And what about you, Sayeed? giggled Bilal.

Don't you guys know anything about capitalism yet? Sayeed looked back and forth between the two with a devious smile. *See that airplane you guys are working on? I'm the guy who OWNS the motherfucker*, he laughed out loud, *Now get to work!*

The warm spring sun was shining down on them. It shone on Sayeed, who had grabbed the tray and was pretending to bang Bilal over the head with it. And the sun shone on Bilal, kneeling in the dust, slapping his hands with laughter on the road. And on Naseem too, who picked up his oud, and began to improvise a little song about airlines, money, and unrequited love. For an instant, that's all there was in the world—sunlight and laughter and song—it filled their ears and became eternal, just for that one moment.

Bilal finally got up and dusted himself off and then took the tray back from Sayeed. *Come on,* he told his brother, *it's time to go meet Baba.* Naseem scooted himself down from the wall, landing on his feet. *Yallah!*

Why don't you come with us, Sayeed?

Not today, Sayeed answered. The two of them walked him home. Christine and Lydia were standing in the doorway, drinking tea.

In a cheerful voice, Bilal called out, *Hey, sisters!* Lydia smiled and waved. Christine scowled.

In God's name, it's wrong to carry a grudge, Bilal shouted out, offering Christine an insolent smile. Then as the brothers moved off down the street, they started clapping and chanting a popular patriotic song:

> *I am my brother*
> *I am my brother*
> *I believe in the people, lost and chained*

> *And I carry my gun*
> *So the next generation*
> *May carry their sickles again*

Lydia listened and watched them go. *Hey, comrades,* she called them back. *Come on. I have something for you.* She quickly ran inside and brought out a pile of freshly baked spinach pies wrapped in a cloth napkin. She put them into Naseem's hands. *Here, brother, God keep you.*

They accepted the pastries and walked away, turning twice to grin and wave their thanks. Out of modesty they walked out of sight, around the corner, before they opened the napkin. How long had it been since they had eaten something like this? Months, years, a lifetime? Before they had reached the last corner before the check post, they had gobbled the spinach pies down, squabbling like children over the last crumbs.

This is what the Aseelah family understood about Tel Zaatar camp: It was a place in grave danger. Filled with Palestinian fighters, it was situated at a strategic point in the city on the edge of Christian-controlled East Beirut. The Aseelah family understood and foresaw the tragedy.

In the coming summer the Tel Zaatar refugee camp would be surrounded on all sides. No food and water would be allowed in through the cordon, the electricity shut off, people inside the camp would begin to starve. Just to get water from the camp's water supply would become a daily journey toward death. A rain of bullets would fall down on whoever tried to fetch water for the others. Caged like animals, even civilians would be shot down like sparrows by Phalangist snipers if they tried to escape.

Sayeed's family decided to get out before the siege became the horrific nightmare that it, in fact, turned out to be.

Early in the year there had been a sign of the coming disaster. The news came of the massacre of Karantina. The whole neighborhood, filled with poor Lebanese Muslims and Palestinian refugees, had been laid to waste. Then two days later came the reprisal. The coastal village of Damour was attacked by the leftist alliance, and most Christian inhabitants were evicted, many killed.

The Aseelah family knew that Tel Zaatar was next on the list. They felt certain that the occasional blast in the camp would soon turn into a full-blown blockade. By late spring, the Aseelah family was determined to leave.

I think our best bet is to move up to Jounieh, Christine announced one morning at breakfast. They were all sitting at the table drinking tea, eating a simple meal of bread with olive oil and zaatar. Christine's announcement took everyone by surprise. Jounieh was a port town north of Beirut, the Maronite capital.

Oh for God's sake, Christine, Lydia practically shrieked. *Do you know what you're saying?* Many were the stories of Palestinians hanged, dragged, knifed, and thrown in the dry riverbed at Jounieh.

I know some very good people who have gone up there. I think we'd be safe, Christine said calmly.

If we leave at all, we'll head south, said Lydia, *to Tyre or Sidon*. For her part, she also had good reason to want to be there. It was a bastion of leftist guerrillas, both Lebanese and Palestinian.

Tyre! Now that's out of the frying pan and into the fire, injected Moussa cynically.

Are we even in agreement that we should leave? asked Lydia. *Think of the thousands of others who can't leave.*

Anyone who wants to be lined up against a wall and shot down like the people in Karantina can stay, said Moussa.

Sayeed who had been very quiet during all of this finally spoke up. *I have decided to stay here and defend the camp with my friends*, he said quietly. *They are planning to join the struggle, and so am I.*

Oh no, said Moussa cutting him off. *Oh no. You'll come wherever we go.*

You can't decide for me. You're not my father.

No, I'm not, but we're not going to let you die like your father.

If not to Jounieh, then let's just take a flat in Ashrafiyeh. Christine was pushing for them to take up residence in any Christian quarter. Even Moussa thought this was an outrageous suggestion, considering the fact that Ashrafiyeh was now the front line.

I guess you are convinced that the revolution is destined to fail? Lydia pointed her question at her sister. Christine left it alone and turned to her mother.

Mother? What do you say?

The older woman sighed and put her forehead in the palms of her hands, shaking it back and forth. *How many wars do we have to flee? Our brothers and sisters in Lebanon and Syria should be fighting with us, not against us…* she kept shaking her head in despair.

Everyone remained quiet, waiting for her to continue. *But you youngsters know this country better than I. I'm a stranger.*

Just then the kitchen shook violently with a loud series of explosions in the vicinity. For several seconds the entire house moved, the table jumped; the windowpanes rattled loudly in their frames. Sayeed ran to the front window to see what had been hit. A thick black cloud of smoke was rising from the direction of the check post. In an instant, Sayeed was out the door and running.

It's hours past midnight, and Khalid is walking east on the Boulevard, in a city at the edge of the sea, ten thousand miles from his past lives. As he walks, Khalid remembers it all. But it's not a memory distant and long gone. He feels alive in it right now. A burning sensation, an actual pain right under his skin. There is no gap between present and memory. No chain of events that makes sense. No moment that he can pinpoint and say, "that's the past" and "now it's over." He feels, right this instant, a knife in his spleen, the severing of bodies, the wailing of mourners. It's all lumped together: running away from the camp, the waves of refugees, Sabra and Shatila, the charred bodies he himself pulled from a collapsed building in 1982.

The bombing of Baghdad right now seems just an extension of those earlier wars. To him, it's all one history, one experience, one endless story. '48, '56, '67, '73, '75 '82, and now, '91—all the same war, and he's living Beirut all over again. When Khalid hears of the thousands of American "sorties," he is not impressed with the popular jargon. He has been on the other side of the falling bombs.

Khalid has never been able to admit to himself the guilt he feels, that he—by some stroke of luck—was able to survive while so many around him perished. Thousands of ordinary people just like him. And he feels a secret gnawing guilt that he himself never took up arms to defend the innocents who were being slaughtered around him. This harrowing guilt is buried inside.

Sometimes he used to wake up in the middle of the night and look at Irene sleeping next to him. He'd see not a mate, but a complete outsider to all of this. Sometimes he hated himself for falling in love with her. It felt like a betrayal of his past. Why did he leave Beirut? He should have married a Palestinian woman, someone who shared these wounds inside him.

He would stay awake gazing at Irene and often feel resentful—of her growing domesticity, her privilege, her ability to cheerfully hum little songs around the house. And then a few minutes later, when he couldn't take his alienation any more, he'd finally reach out and whisper to her: *I'm empty, Irene. I don't feel good anymore.*

Usually she'd wake up with him and drink tea until dawn. And listen to the fragmented bits and pieces that made up his life, whichever piece he was inclined to tell. Once he told her the story of an old woman in his village who placed a single almond in his hand right after his parents died, as if it were a golden charm. The woman closed the fingers of his hand around the almond and whispered a prayer over his closed fist. *Don't worry, my son, you won't be alone.*

Khalid told Irene too about the beauty of his grandfather's ancient olive groves on the hill behind the village, their silvery leaves dancing in the breeze. In the fall the villagers harvested the olives, cured and pickled them, pressed the oil—always pitching in together, always lending a hand. Always bearing any burden together, shoulder to shoulder.

And Irene always stayed and listened to these memories, and talked until the sun rose again.

Khalid walks now, remembering these nights spent awake. He is forced to say to himself that, yes, she had been good to him. Over the years, she had been the one to stand by him, to listen, and even to challenge him to be a better person.

He had always thought that he would live in a world in which the oppressed and oppressor were clearly defined. But that wasn't right, was it? Here was Irene, beautiful Irene, a part of his enemy's world, and yet different. She had even learned to speak his language.

As Khalid now walks along, thinking, reflecting, he spots a parked van humming by the side of the road. A young black man jumps down from the truck with a bundle of morning newspapers that he's delivering to the newsstand.

Mind if I see one of those? Khalid asks the deliveryman.

No problem, the guy hands him the top paper in the stack.

Thanks, brother, Khalid says, then adds, *We are all brothers.*

Got that right, the youth says with a smile. He hops back up behind the wheel and adds, *Take it easy, bro.*

After the van departs, Khalid looks down at the headline and picture. They grab him and do not let him go.

As soon as Sayeed heard the explosion outside the house in Tel Zaatar, he ran. He ran out the door and down the street. Past graffiti on cement, trash piles, and posters of martyrs on the walls, past a mother calling out anxiously for her child. Sayeed ran, and all the things of the world became ghostlike and translucent as he dashed toward the edge of the camp.

When he arrived at the scene there was a flurry of

activity. The whole top of the office building was missing and the rest on fire. People were running around screaming. A man bumped into Sayeed and practically knocked him over as he pulled a wounded woman out of the rubble. Through the smoke and the chaos, Sayeed saw two bodies lying side by side on the street. He rushed over to look at their charred faces.

My god, he screamed, and dived closer. Naseem's arm was blown off, hanging by a thread of flesh. Bilal's leg the same. Both of their faces were blackened, charred; their mouths, gaping open, teeth bared, as if their last words had been screams of pain. Sayeed wailed as he collapsed on top of them, hiding their faces, even from himself. He wrapped himself around his friends, trying to protect them from what had already happened. He had no control then and no memory later of what happened next. Voices around him disappeared.

Mama, he whimpered. It was the only word that could come out of his mouth, *Mama, mama,* as he cradled his own face in his hands and sobbed.

He lifted his head for a minute and looked around him. Everything was a slow-motion blur. As if time had stopped that very moment. As if time had stopped, but everything else was still moving. People had become nothing more than shadows. He heard nothing. Didn't even see that his cousin Lydia had followed him down from the house and was standing above him. He didn't hear her screaming, *God! Oh my God!* He looked straight at her, and yet didn't see her at all. And then he looked down at his friends again.

All over again, he was weeping, not just for them but suddenly for the fact of being a Palestinian. He saw in front of his eyes the whole picture, the whole story. He saw the history of his own family before his eyes, as if lined up and projected on a wall. *Why?* He cried out. *Why?* In an instant he saw the loss of his own parents, and how he had grown up without them. He stared again at his two best friends' bodies.

He dropped his face into Bilal's chin, breathed in deeply, smelled his odor, which still had something alive in it—the smell of dirt and sweat. Like a rush of judgment, like a stream of curses, the entire world came tumbling inward on him. He felt the whole world crumbling, suffocating him with pure weight. At that very moment, the moment of breaking, Lydia's voice finally reached him, *You've got to be strong, Sayeed. There's nothing you can do for them now. They are martyrs.* He thought that it must be Aunt Salwa speaking to him. *Be strong, Habibi,* he heard his Aunt's voice say to him. He envisioned her warm eyes in front of him and it calmed him. He lifted his eyes again, but when he looked out at the world around him, it had changed. It would never be the same again.

Within a few days, his family would leave their home and he would go with them bitterly. They were taking refuge in the far west of Beirut right along the beach. They had each packed a small suitcase, sorting through all the papers that proved ownership of the house and the properties, bank records, and other documents. From the living room wall, Sitti Mary took down the framed picture of her husband, Aisa, and held it up to the light. *We won't leave you behind,* she said to his face and packed the picture into her suitcase.

They had no way of knowing that they would never see their home again. For the second time, they became refugees. In August, Tel Zaatar would be destroyed in a grisly rampage that lasted for days. When the radios announced the fall of the camp, the ensuing massacre, and that not a single Palestinian fighter was left alive in the camp, even Christine was crying inconsolably. From that day forward, she never said another word against Lydia or the fighters or their cause.

Khalid sinks to his knees under a streetlight with the newspaper in his hand. He stares at the headline: *Civilian Shelter Hit in Baghdad; Hundreds Feared Dead.* He looks at the woman's face in the picture in front of the shelter. The shape of her face, the expression in her eyes looks so familiar to him. It could be a cousin, an aunt, his own mother. He feels the sea of tears, pressing at the wall behind his eyes— the Red Sea, the Dead Sea, al Mutawwaset, the Sea of Galilee—where *al-Messih* once walked on water.

It's been fifteen years since Khalid has allowed any break in that wall. He thought he was holding everything together. But now he finds out that he is holding nothing together, in fact that he is nothing. He's not a thing, or a being, or even a person. He feels more like a blank location. An empty shell, a shifting place where history meets absence and the wreckage of the past.

A small trickle of wetness appears on Khalid's cheek. He reaches to wipe it, not even knowing how it got there, or where it came from. He wipes it away vaguely with his sleeve, expecting to be done with it.

But then another drop of water leaks out of his eye and rolls down his cheek. And he wipes it too. And then another. And each time he wipes the wetness away, another droplet forms to take its place.

Shit, he says to himself with a tremor in his voice, *I'm losing it.*

Then he does. With the newspaper dated February 14, 1991 on the ground in front of him, with a pair of eyes reaching him from far away, he breaks down into tears, a long spasm of choked gasps and sobs. And in the midst of his wails and weeping, he finally forgets everything, everything except the one word that is written inside this curtain of tears.

14
A Chapter of Her Own

Irene was reclining in bed with the window open above her. It was night. A breeze was ruffling the white gauze curtains. Like a beam of liquid moonlight, Khalid slipped soundlessly through the window. He came in silently and began to comb her hair. He combed it, not with an actual comb, but with poetry, and each line of poetry was one tooth of the comb, smoothing her hair, smoothing everything into place.

The words he murmured were soft and repetitive, like raindrops, like cushioned footsteps, like the drone of bees in summer, a translucent architecture of sounds that made sense only when heard from a place far within an inner ear.

Khalid breathed lines of poetry and whispered them with his fingers, and lulled them through her hair. She thought she grasped a meaning. She wanted to ask him if it was true. But she somehow knew that it was against the rules to speak.

When Khalid slipped back out the window and disappeared again, she found herself awake, in the same room, with the same open window. But next to her on the bed there was only moonlight where Khalid had been.

Irene woke with a sensation of tranquil intimacy, but instantly it was ruptured by the memory of the fight that she and Khalid had had just hours before. He had ended the whole thing by crashing his beer bottle against the wall, and storming out the door. *I'm getting out of here*, were his last words. *I'm getting out* was still shooting through her head like lightning and thunder.

The scathing echoes of his words returned to make her recoil once more. *This is not a war. This is a massacre. Desert Storm? Where did they get that metaphor? This is not a storm. People, children are dying. But that means nothing to you.*

His words shredded the remains of the beautiful, mystical dream. Two images, two representations of Khalid were fighting for ascendancy in her mind. Who was Khalid anyway? Was he the angelic figure who floated like moonlight, murmuring poetry into her dream life? Or was he the anguished man, unable to repress his pent-up bitterness.

But as she lay there thinking about what he had said, she had to admit that he was right in some ways—about the war, the ignorance and hatred filling the air around them. But was Khalid right about her, too? Irene wondered. At first the answer seemed to be no. Wasn't she a dissident? Wasn't she critical of the ruling ideology? Hadn't she marched, spoken at rallies, written articles against the war?

When Khalid had screamed his words at her earlier in the night, she experienced them not as words, but rather as weapons used against her; and so they didn't mean anything to her. They were simply senseless utterances, shouted in anger, fired like bullets—to be deflected at all cost.

But as she lay there in bed, Irene now began to absorb them; she began to feel their wounds. A gnawing feeling took over, and her stomach felt raw and empty. *People, children are dying but that means nothing to you*, he had said.

Irene's mind jumped back to an evening they had spent at Sarah's house almost a year earlier. Jules had recently left Sarah to go and live permanently in the south of France. Right after he left, Sarah called Khalid and asked them both to spend some time with her.

All evening long, Khalid talked with Sarah about Jules'

departure. Irene was again amazed at Khalid's agility with consoling words, his ability to touch the painful subject with his hands, molding the matter like clay, offering up shapes that both Irene and Sarah recognized as powerful and true. He never spoke of his dislike of Jules, but rather emphasized his love and respect for Sarah.

What became clear to Irene that evening was that Khalid was—unlike herself—in a moral position to speak openly to Sarah about her life. He had never hurt Sarah. He had never lied to her or desired her husband. They had always and only met as equals. But then Khalid was like that with everyone. With Mounir. With Kathy, even with Jules himself. Though he didn't like Jules, he never pretended that he did either. He didn't get enmeshed in vague, ambiguous relationships with people.

In my part of the world, he told Sarah and Irene that night, *we have a saying that you hear all the time: "Il y bidou ynzil min al Samaa, bidha t'itlaqa al ard." Whatever the sky sends down, the earth has to take. Or "the earth will absorb." It actually has a positive message. Whatever fate brings, the earth can handle it. WE will survive.*

Later that night in bed Irene told him of her admiration for his eloquence. *Maturity*, he said, *is knowing what to say at the right time.*

It's about making choices, he continued. *In the great Power-Desire continuum that we used to argue about. If you don't make clear choices, you end up with neither desire nor power. You'll be afraid of your own shadow.*

But what did any of this have to do with his terrible explosion against her? What sin had she committed to make him hurl all the wrong words at the wrong time?

Still in her bed thinking these thoughts, Irene listened to the house to see if Khalid had come home while she was sleeping. She looked at the clock. It was three a.m. She listened intently. There was no sound.

She got out of bed, slipped on a robe, and went to see for

certain that he wasn't sleeping on the couch. He was not
there. Where was he? At a friend's house? Drinking coffee at
Denny's? Walking? Gone forever?

The phone suddenly rang, piercing the silence. It startled
Irene, but then her heart skipped a beat. She rushed to the
bedroom to answer.

Allo, said an accented voice. Irene immediately
recognized Khalid's Aunt Salwa.

Allo. Irene responded in the Arabic way.

Irene?

Ah, ah, Irene affirmed. Her Arabic was getting better and
she could now muddle through some basic conversations. *Fi
ishi?* Irene asked. *Is there anything wrong?* This was always
the first question Khalid asked whenever his aunt called,
especially if the call arrived in the middle of the night.

Nothing new under the sun, habibti, Salwa said, *We're
under curfew because of this cursed war...I just wanted to
hear Sayeed's voice.*

Khalid mish mawjoud. Irene said abruptly. There was a
pause after Irene spoke.

Where is he, dear? A silence arose between the two
women.

I don't know. He left earlier and hasn't come back. Irene
wasn't sure if she was making sense in Arabic.

*Isma'i Irene. If you and Sayeed are having a fight, don't
worry. It'll be okay.* Irene said nothing.

Irene, Salwa continued very slowly, pronouncing each
syllable. *Inti dahabi.*

Shoo "dahabi?" Irene asked.

Salwa tried to explain in English. *You're like gold, ya
habibti. Like a piece of gold.* Salwa pronounced "piece" with
a "b" instead of a "p." *A biece of gold.* Salwa switched back
to Arabic again. *When Sayeed comes home, tell him to call
me. Take care.*

Salwa's voice soon drifted away into the night; and the
warmth of Salwa's reassuring words in Irene's ears soon

dropped to room temperature again. Irene felt even more isolated than before.

This was how it always was. Both Khalid's and her own family arrived only as disembodied voices—an occasional letter or phone call. They visited in waves of sound, or lines of ink, not as a physical presence or an embrace. They came through the air, through wires, by satellite, or in lightweight envelopes marked *Par Avion.*

Always the sense of abandonment. Always the silence in the middle of the night.

Dahabi, Irene wrote down a notepad next to the phone, next to the words: *Salwa called. Call her back.* Irene did her best to write the new word using the Arabic alphabet. But she wasn't sure which of the two h's to use. Was it the normal h or the aspirated h?

Alone and awake at night, Irene knew that she would not be able to sleep again. She decided to make herself a cup of tea. As she walked to the kitchen, she spied the broken shards of glass from Khalid's beer bottle next to the wall. She walked over, reaching down to clean them up. But just then she changed her mind, leaving them where they were.

In the kitchen, she switched on the gas beneath the kettle, and put on a Bob Dylan tape to keep herself company while waiting for the water to boil. Dylan was singing *Tangled up in Blue* when Irene sat down with her tea.

There was a newspaper lying on the floor near the kitchen table with a picture of Nelson Mandela on the back page right next to ads for bras and underwear. A few days earlier had been the one-year anniversary of Mandela's release from prison.

Irene remembered very well the day that he was released. Although she did not even know him, had never seen him, had never been to South Africa, his personal liberation was an intimate event for her. Her body was covered in goose bumps when she watched the scenes on television. Why? Was it for the man himself, or was it because he had become a symbol for everyone, even herself, about the triumph of justice over violence and hatred? Whatever the case, she had lived his cause, had spoken his name often; she felt as though she knew him. And yet she did not.

Irene contemplated the strangeness and even folly of her predicament. She had found herself celebrating the liberation of a freedom fighter fifteen thousand miles away, and yet her own personal life was in a shambles. It was a disgraceful failure. What had really happened, after all, to make everything beautiful turn to hell?

Dylan was still singing. *You hurt the ones that I loved best; you covered up the truth with lies. One day you'll be in the ditch, flies buzzing round your eyes, blood on your saddle*...His caustic words rang out from the tape player, pulling Irene towards their brutal finality.

She looked often toward the door, hoping that Khalid would walk through it at any moment. She imagined that he would arrive like the warm Santa Ana winds in the middle of winter, that he would come in through the window as he had in the dream, bearing no rancor, only gifts of affectionate words. That he would come and hold her and that in one embrace they would erase three years of mistakes. But he did not.

When the teacup was empty and the tape had clicked to a stop, Irene turned off the lights and moved over to the couch. She wrapped herself in an old sleeping bag that had been left on the floor. Cowering in the dark, she stared out the window, listening to the sound of the cottage creaking. Listening again to the voices that were playing inside of her.

There were no distractions now to relieve her of a clear picture of the venomous exchange the night before.

Khalid was standing above her, near the window. She was sitting right on this very couch.

You act as though everything's that's wrong with the world is my *fault!*

No, I act like everything that's wrong with the world is wrong with you too!

She could hear Khalid's precise tonality, the way his eyes looked when he said those words. His countenance resembled a missile more than a human face. Irene held her breath and put her head down on her knees. It was awful to confront the truth. She had been too proud or ashamed to admit it. Yes, she did know what he was talking about. Never mind whatever he had done wrong. She always used whatever HE had done to exonerate herself from what SHE herself had done. And now she clearly saw the truth—that she too had been cowardly, that she too hadn't risked enough, hadn't crossed boundaries, hadn't really learned how to love.

Why were they unable to stop the hemorrhaging between them that was bleeding them both to death? As she looked back down the avenue of the years, she saw the clear path of destruction from their first summer together all the way until this moment. Yes, there were good times, but they never lasted. And every time Irene had a chance to change, to get closer to Khalid, to help their love flourish and bloom, she had failed. Not just him. She had dragged her own past and his past sins around like a moldy, moth-eaten blanket.

Irene began to cry soft tears.

Years earlier, when her neighbor Stefano had attacked her in his condo near the beach, he actually sent her a thank-you card in the mail. It was one of those Chinese cards depicting art from the Ming era. With a gilt background, bamboo, and red flowers; the image exuded a kind of spiritual calm. On the back of the card it said, *Thank you for a lovely evening. Let's do it again.*

Irene didn't throw that card into the trash. Instead she tucked it away into a box full of letters and mementos. She kept that card for years, and looked at it from time to time. Why? Was it because the gilded image was so beautiful? Or was it because she had an obsession for keeping every scrap of paper that had ever passed through her hands? Or did it stand as some kind of false proof that nothing bad really happened after all? What happened was that she had somehow consented to the postcard's lie.

This was the very kind of thing that drove Khalid crazy. *How could you keep a souvenir from an obscene asshole?* he wondered when he saw her sorting through the box of papers. She hadn't understood why it made him so angry, so angry that she had kept it. To him it was incomprehensible. There was only one existential path: categorical rejection of oppression.

Had she learned anything at all since those days? She still seemed to be ruled by an instinct to ignore the bad parts of life so that they might simply disappear. Perhaps she had hoped that if she ignored Khalid's pain, it would simply go away on its own. How absent had she been? How blind?

Blindness. Hadn't she said it all those years ago? *It's like the blind leading the blind*, she said to Bernie once on the phone. She had been blind to Bernie's pain, and then her own, and now Khalid's too. It was a blindness typical of her whole people, wasn't it? *They can't see what they are doing around the world, or they just don't want to. And I am not any better than they are. Blind.*

If she had been able to truly see herself and him, perhaps she could have guided both of them to higher ground. As it was, she was unable to pull either one of them to a safer place. This was the thing that was shameful—that she had allowed them both to wander so long in that lonely desert.

Irene shivered. The soft tears turned into bitter tears of regret. *It's you, Irene,* she lamented out loud, *you, you, you.* There was an endless ache in her stomach as if she'd been kicked repeatedly by an enraged horse, until she was practically unable to breathe. *You broke everything.* She held her head tight so that it would not split apart.

All of her many heroes, from Mandela to Malcolm, appeared in a line in front of her as little figurines. Small, frozen statuettes—motionless and cold. Of what use were they now to her? They could only mean something to those who had the ability to emulate their struggles. *Little figurines, she scoffed bitterly to herself out loud. Little figurines.*

Before her very eyes, she saw them each come to life, one by one, and march away out of reach.

Come back, she screamed to them, but they were already gone.

Come back! She screamed this time, not to the little icons, but to another figment of her imagination, and that was Khalid.

Come back, she whispered and collapsed again, pulling the sleeping bag over her head.

I still love you, you schmuck, she said in a muffled tone from beneath the bag. Her voice echoed in her ears. Hearing her own raspy voice utter the word *schmuck*, she started to laugh—a hoarse laugh. For this was the word that they had often called each other when they were only slightly annoyed with each other. When he had washed a bright red sock in with her white underwear, she called him *schmuck.* When she had promised to do the dishes and then left them instead for an onslaught of ants: *schmuckeroo.* When he ate the last bit of ice cream that, in all fairness, should have been hers— *double schmuck!*

*You criminal, you rogue, you...*Irene called out again, her voice rising from the nest of the ancient sleeping bag. Though she was alone in the cottage, part penitent on her knees at the altar, part raving lunatic, she still tried to think of the exact right word to describe him:

Incorrigible
Temperamental
Inflexible
Obstinate
Obdurate
Demanding
Incessant

She trotted briskly all the way down that road; when she reached the very end, she was forced to turn around and saunter back up the same road but in the other direction:

Memorable
Gentle
Generous
Yielding
Resourceful
Principled
Whimsical

Eternal, she added an extra word to the list.

She found herself thinking about Khalid's ability to make words flutter, his gift for producing a feast from an empty fridge, for exhuming a breath of humor from a dull day, for making history from everyday life.

I still love you, she thought to herself, *I who have fallen from a loveless tree, in a loveless landscape.*

This was the very thing she had been wondering for such a long time. Did she still even have the ability to love at all? This was the question that had taken every size and shape, and that was the origin of all the uncertainty that Khalid had been able to taste in every one of her kisses. And which drove him utterly mad. But despite everything, she did love him.

Because no matter what had happened between them, it did not lack meaning. And, in the end, that was what mattered. It might take a historian, a sage, a novelist, or a god to determine what the hell that meaning was. But there was meaning, and she knew that.

Irene now remembered the image of Khalid pouring in the window like liquid gold, combing poetry into her hair. Whispering clandestine syllables into her ear. She now saw that it was not Khalid's poetry at all, but her own. She realized that this vision was her own creation, her own desires which had unrolled before her like a carpet of joy. She had this power. To make the invisible become visible again. Even as the world sank into its cold violence, she could conjure moonlight and gardens made of regret and loss.

Earlier, when she woke up, the verses in the dream had been an indistinct blur, a murmur of indecipherable sounds. Now the sounds began to take form. She went to find a pencil and a paper and began to write down the lines that began as if already written onto an interior page.

> *Peace, I loved you*
> *like a storm*
>
> *And all the joys of a childhood*
> *among flowers come back*
>
> *with a sword*
>
> *at the sight of sweet magnolia*
> *saltwater drains across face and*
>
> *I admit I was the last one*
> *to trade in my arms.*

* * *

Long ago there was a beautiful young man with dark eyes and dark curls with a broad smile on his face. He was grinning from ear to ear because he had just met the woman of his life. How did he know this? He felt the buzzing of ten thousand bees beneath every inch of his skin. When he reached out to hold her hand, it felt as though he was reaching for a part of himself that had been missing since he was six years old.

And there was a young woman poised anxiously on the edge of discovery. What was she longing to discover? Not just love, but a whole part of herself that she had not yet been able to locate, a treasure that had been stolen from her while she was still half-asleep.

As they walked together one April day to a bar called "The Escape," the man grabbed her hand, and held it in his. Southern California had never looked so welcoming. Purple jacaranda blossoms seemed to accept him with open arms; the palm trees were hovering like guardian angels over everything, the blessed scent of Mexico was coming up from the soil.

As they reached the corner, their bodies drew closer, until all space between them disappeared. She turned to look at him and brought her lips to his ear.

I think I love you, Khalid, she said, pronouncing his name just right. He pulled back and looked into her eyes, searching them. He looked at her candid, open face, studying it. He looked into her soul; and recognized it. *My lover is blue ocean, the unknown next, the joy of songs, the tears of the unsayable*.

Cars were passing by, people were strolling past, the world around him was rolling towards its own separate fate. But he was careening ever more quickly towards his own. *I love you*, he spoke—a vow that wouldn't be broken. They were drawn into a kiss that almost brought them to the pavement with rapture. They melted into each other's shape, became one, and forgot that they had only met that very afternoon.

This is the way it happened. They never did go to meet Mounir for that drink at the bar. Instead they ditched him and went skipping together towards the park. They dashed in and out between the trees, chased each other, and played like children in the grass. He let her catch him as often as she wanted. She let him trap her on the ground with the length of his body. They looked into each others' eyes fearlessly, with smiles that reached all the way back into the throat and beyond.

This is the way it happened. And this is the way Khalid remembers it. This is the story that Khalid tells himself as he opens the door to their cottage just before dawn, after his long night alone.

Irene, he says softly. To himself. He doesn't wish to wake her from where she has fallen asleep on the couch. He is only confirming something for himself. *Irene,* he repeats again. Yes, this is the word that always dances with the two dark spots behind his eyes. It swims in his blood, and travels with him wherever he goes.

The cottage is exactly as he left it. The shattered bottle of beer is still on the floor where he threw it many hours before. He cringes at the thought of his stupid, outrageous outburst, and kneels down to pick up the pieces of the bottle.

When the mess is finally cleaned up, including the beer that had splashed on the carpet and trickled down the wall, he walks over to the couch and reaches to brush Irene's face with the back of his fingers. She wakes and immediately reads his tender expression. They look into each other's eyes for a long silent moment.

I've been wrong, he finally says to her.

No, it's me, she says vehemently, but he interrupts her.

All night I've been thinking. I've been thinking about Bilal and Naseem, he pauses and then his voice wavers. *And I realized...*

But Irene doesn't let him finish; she holds out her arms and lets him come in. And there is no need for either of them to say anything. Their mouths and limbs and organs take them where words are unable to travel.

Later on in the day when Khalid returns Salwa's midnight phone call, she tells him this: *Love isn't a choice, my dear one, it's a fate.*

15
The Woman I Left Behind

You never finish telling a story, Khalid said.

How can you say that? Irene was surprised.

Every time you start to tell one, it gets cut short. Nothing ever happens.

What happens is that my thoughts unfold, my words and spirit are released. It's called poetry.

Why don't you tell a story from beginning to end for a change?

She was quiet. She was also exhausted. Sarah had left only a little while earlier after a long planning meeting. It was April, and they were starting a campaign to help several families rebuild their destroyed homes in Bethlehem. The three of them had been doing more and more political organizing lately. They worked well together, and a bond was forming between them that seemed to transcend all of their mutual history.

What are you afraid of? Khalid asked and touched Irene's face. She pulled back.

Nothing. I'm just not a storyteller at heart. I've got too poor a memory. Too weak an imagination. Besides, I never know where to start.

Would it be easier if I disappeared? I'll pretend I'm not

me. You can pretend it's not you. He pulled way back into the shadows of the room. And she pulled into her own shadow.

There was silence again.

How many evenings did they spend like this in the dark—telling stories, talking, crying? It seemed like a century had gone by. A century of passages through sleepless nights, oceans of swaying wheat, broken promises. There was the sound of a dog barking in the distance, the ghostly presence of a white cross gleaming on the mountain behind them, and then came her voice:

This is a story that takes place a long time ago. I've told you parts before, fragments. You know it already. It's called "The Woman I Left Behind." Irene thought for a moment, then began:

Once upon a time she was sitting on a beach trying to construct dreams from nightmares, trying to create a self from scratch. To passersby, she might have looked like an appealing innocent, clasping her knees in the sand.

Wait, Khalid interrupted. *Who's the "she" in the story?*

I thought you were going to pretend you weren't here? Irene asked in a grouchy voice.

Sorry. I won't say another word.

Now you've broken the mood. I have to start over.

Sorry, he mumbled again. Then he lit a cigarette. Oddly enough, this was a good sign, a sign that he was prepared to be quiet for a while. Irene began again:

Once upon a time she was sitting on a beach trying to construct dreams from nightmares.

Once she was sobbing to the tune of Bob Marley while a pink penis bobbed closer and closer to her face.

Once she was so hungry she stole an apple from an orange, the orange from its neighbor in a basket. Once too, she believed that she was a god who was crucified for nothing, for absolutely nothing. But all that time she knew there was a real god named No God; and that she lived in the center of its expanding absence.

The woman I left behind was wearing tight white cotton pants and an aqua blue jersey on the day I left her. Her dirty blond hair—long and shapeless—hung in druthers around her pale white face. She was nineteen at the time, but even then she was a wisp in my mind, so absent and airy that she was gone before I even knew her, before I had a chance to say goodbye. When I would look straight at her, I saw only palm trees swaying behind her and the open sky. And whenever I try to think of her now—just images of empty beer bottles, pink curlers, scattered pills—no memory of her face.

The woman I left behind was invisible to herself and others. It was as if her aching mind, always trying to escape, was making an atom of her—restless—too small to be seen. She had taken her high school graduation money and bought a ticket to California. For two years she lived at the level of survival.

Her family was on the East Coast, but ever since her childhood they had always let her down, was what she'd always said. Her father was a rich, successful something or other. Her mother was obsessed with things like linen—wore tailored suits with matching pumps and pearls everywhere she went. At a certain point the woman just stopped trusting them. So even their occasionally good advice was useless to her. So were their phone calls—useless—on birthdays and holidays.

"How are you doing?" they'd say over three thousand miles of silent wire. The most she could ever do was wait, then whisper," fine," over her end of the line; and then after a few more moments of silence, hang up. She was ever alone with herself and her endless emotions.

She saw them as painted balloons, floating beyond her reach. But the truth was, she was the one that had flown from them, never to return. The truth was that they were not the people she had painted them to be. She had eyes that wouldn't work, and couldn't see that they were just as human as she.

When I dream about her now, she is always trapped inside a dark car, pounding on the window, screaming, "Please! God! Don't leave me!" As if the car was on fire. But in my waking life, I can barely remember her at all, can't even picture her features.

I do remember the time she was standing at the corner near the park at Sixth Avenue, watching traffic. The gardens behind her were in full spring bloom—magnolias, tulips, varicolored azaleas. But she just stood there facing the intersection, staring at the cars going by. She was saying how America is like a cat's paw: sometimes a paw but beneath it all—a claw.

One day she was sitting alone on a windy beach, trying to meditate, or at least to think a private thought. But the contents of her brain, like a solar eclipse, were too painful to look at directly. A mirror held up to the underside of her thoughts reflected warped images:

> Vibrant, lunatic color of burning water. A danger so cold. If you see a passing storm. Cool twill is not a warm region. We are at war always at war. Winter is icummin. Winter. So wide can't get over it. So low can't get around it. Insurmountable freeze, I think my body is, but the spirit is always talking to another who is not here and is nothing...because it is the center of nothing.

And so she sat on the cold damp sand, wanting to pull something good out of terrible chaos. Just at this moment two men walked up the shoreline and plopped themselves down next to her.

Actually she had seen them approaching, eyeing her. She was hoping that they would just leave her alone. And yet she knew they wouldn't and, of course, they didn't. The two were already seated when the first one spoke in a Southern drawl:

"Hi, I'm Jay and this is Todd. Mind if we sit here?"

"Well, I do, I'm busy," she replied.

"Well, you don't look busy," said the other man with a similar Southern tone.

"Well, I aaaam busy," she said, drawing out her vowels in light mockery of their accents.

"Okay, but can we just ask you one question? See we've got this bet going," said one, "that you would come smoke a joint with us. I was the one who said you would, so you have to. Come on..."

She knew she was already gone. She only recognized herself when she was failing at something, or letting others use her, or flat drunk watching the ceiling fan go in circles and circles. People came and went in her life—all shadows. No one had a grip. Roommates, friends, roommates' friends, friends of roommates' friends all passed through her life, a vision on the perimeter of things. And so did men, and she let them.

"What's your name, sweetheart?" one said passing the joint to her. They had succeeded in getting her to their apartment. Several posters of bikini-clad women were the only attempt at a décor. A fat metal clock was ticking on the dingy wall.

"I don't have one anymore," she said inhaling the sweet weed with the squinted eyes of a pro. The two hands on the loud ticking clock said ten to two in the afternoon.

"Names are only for those with a home and a place," she said.

"That's very, very interesting," said the man whose name was Jay, "Okay, no-name-girl, that's fine, fine. I'm just going to go put on some tunes."

Just then the other one, Todd, walked in from the kitchen and sat down next to her saying,, "I brought you a nice big drink so we can get to know each other better." At this she gave out a shockingly loud hoot. Then she took another hit from the joint, then another, and another. Sunshine was pouring through the only window onto a plant on the sill. It was a fake one, she knew.

The man put his arm around her shoulders and asked her, "So where are you from, then?" She leaned forward, away from his arm, to pick up the drink from the coffee table. It was cold and felt good in her hands. Sipping it for a long while, she closed her eyes. It was a strong rum and Coke. "Cuba Libre," she said out loud to herself and took a few more puffs of the joint.

All of a sudden, everything became faint and discombobulated. A whir of noise and dizziness. She closed her eyes and leaned back, saying, "Shit! What did you put in that joint? What's going on?" She was wearing white pants and an aqua blue jersey, I remember. She leaned back on a brown velour couch with the two men hovering near her. Her head rocked back and forth on the cushion.

"That's right, darlin'," said the first guy, as he stretched her legs out on the couch, "Make yourself real comfortable." From a distant room the soft Reggae sounds of Bob Marley began to float into her ears, sounding warped and slow: "Little darlin'...please don't shed no tears.... No woman no cry." These familiar words and rhythms came rolling to her ears, like a slow motion river, rippling reverberating. "Little darlin', don't shed no tears. No woman, no cry...." Leaning back on the couch with her eyes sealed, her thoughts spun into a void filled with sensations:

I and I are no longer with us. Someone is departing, because I can't hold any longer. In the emptiness of this hand. Please from my wrist take this shadow. From my life, this curse. Words, whatever comes from my mouth—I've found—are just noises and sound. My mind walks into absence. I can't handle it. Separation moves through us, tears through us, and someone is departing. Please don't leave me, my God, I can't handle it.

"I can't handle it. I can't handle it," was what she was saying out loud over and over. Her head was rocking back and forth on the couch in the gesture of "No." That is when I started to fly. I realized then that I had to get out. I had to leave her behind. She wasn't listening anymore to anyone, not even to herself. The truth is, no one could help her. I wasn't abandoning her—she was already alone.

"Think I'm just going to call you honey," one of the men said, taking off his shirt, "You look good, honey. Nice tits." He was unzipping his shorts. She was halfway gone, lying on the couch with her eyes closed when the first man came, bare from the waist down saying, "Come here, Todd, sit on her legs..."

Out of it as she was, she could somehow hear the music, which seemed to emerge from a distant place. She was listening to the Reggae beat of Bob Marley in the background and the words: "One love. One heart. Let's get together and feel all right.... Hear the children praying. Hear the children crying.... Let's get together and I will feel all right. Give thanks and praise to the Lord and I will feel all right...."

I call her the woman I left behind because it was my choice to leave on that day. Because she was a stranger, even to me. She was, as they say, detached, and nothing mattered anymore. She hated the world—the destruction and emptiness around her. But she didn't have the strength or the means to fight back. The last thing she said to me was this: "If we are all a likeness of God, and there is no God, then we're just a likeness of nothing but an evil, deranged, painful world."

"This can be freedom," I said to her, fiercely, without even having to speak...but she said, "No," and refused to come.

On that day, she felt the weight of a man straddling her chest, saying, "Open your eyes and take it." Both of the men were trying to hurt and humiliate her. But they were the fools because you can't steal what's already gone. And all that time the music kept playing and tears were rolling out of the corners of her eyes. Not because of what the men were doing, but for the music she was hearing beyond. For that man who, despite everything, continued to sing beautiful songs of love.

By the time Irene finished talking, it was late. The scent from a nearby blossoming orange tree was drifting in through the open window. The smell flooded her and she was reminded of the orange Khalid gave to her several years earlier after the rally. The smell of citrus on that spring day awakened in her things she had never dreamed of before. The fragrant smell of the white blossoms outside the window now brought all those feelings back again.

Khalid was sitting quietly across the room from her. He hadn't spoken for a while. Now he got up and sat next to her on the couch. He placed his right hand on her "love spot," the exact spot on the center of her sternum that he believed was the key to physical compassion between human beings.

Well? she asked.

She saw that he was still thinking and staring down at his hand on her chest. Finally he broke the silence. *So where did she go?* he asked, *is she gone forever?*

I don't know, Khalid. It's a paradox.

I think I've seen her around.

Where? Irene said in a perplexed voice. *Where?*

I have a picture of her, actually.

Show me.

Khalid got up and walked over to the door of their cottage and took a small mirror from the wall. *Can you handle it?* He gave the mirror to her.

She rolled her eyes at him, but took it despite her reluctance. She glanced down at the small mirror between her hands; her reflection was just visible in the dim light. Blondish hair hung around her face; her lonely gray eyes, devoid of any cosmetics, peered out at her in their usual look of bewilderment. There were the familiar lines around her mouth. Her own lips turned upwards slightly in a half-crooked smile...

What do you see? Khalid asked.

I see myself. Irene kept looking. *I see my lips talking to you now. I see...*

...that you are you, Irene, the woman you were, the woman you are, and the woman you will be. A perfect whole.

Irene looked into the mirror and sighed, *If this is the woman I am going to be, then get me some eyeliner, for god's sake.*

Stop joking around.

I'm not joking...there are some things that I can't leave behind.

And some things, you have. But not yourself, thank god.

What about you? Irene asked, now gripping the mirror. In the room's midnight shadows, she looked at him, focusing on his gentle eyes and parted lips; and she knew that when it came to the really important things, he was always right.

If I were to tell my own story, he finally said, *I would use the same title as yours. "The Woman I Left Behind."*

And who is the woman you left behind?

Without answering, he moved on the couch beside her and placed his cheek next to hers. He clasped his hands onto the mirror over her hands, and together they stared down at the picture they made, cheek to cheek. His dark to her light, his angles to her softer features, his liquid brown eyes to her gray ones—full of questions with no answers.

And who is the woman you left behind? Irene asked again to the reflection of Khalid before her.

I would leave that to the astute reader to figure out. But it's not you. Khalid turned to say this, not to the mirror but to her own face.

Irene didn't know yet, but within days she would find out about the miraculous germination that had already taken place inside of her—the tiny unseen creature who would soon become their first child.

Like everything else they had ever done, they would say *yes* first, and then confront the hard choices and difficult questions later. *Yes,* Khalid would say when they heard the news from the doctor together, *this child already resides in the deepest chambers of my heart.*

Acknowledgments:

I'd like to thank the literary magazines who published some of these chapters in earlier incarnations: *The Long Story, The Toyon Review, Faultline, Emergences,* and *So to Speak.*

Many thanks to the friends and colleagues who offered invaluable suggestions and advice to improve this work: Jodie Rhodes, Kathleen Batcheller, Bobbi Proctor, Susan Muaddi Darraj, Simone Fattal, Ruba Fakhoury, Maren Hackmann, and Joan Jacobson.

A special word of appreciation to my supportive parents, Jim and Karla Jensen, who, thankfully, are almost nothing like the parents described in this book. A shout out to my children, Ahlam and Besan Khamis—they make everything worthwhile. Impossible to forget the unforgettable Zahi Khamis, my husband—whose spirit is present in both the lines and the spaces of this book. Last but not least, nothing but best wishes to the hard-working people at Curbstone for all their wonderful work. Congratulations on thirty years of luminous progressive publishing!

KIM JENSEN is a writer who has lived and taught in California, France, and the Middle East. She and her husband have been active in human rights movements for many years. Her writings have appeared in a wide variety of newspapers and magazines, including *Al Jadid*, *Rain Taxi Review*, *Al-Ahram Weekly*, *Oakland Tribune*, *So to Speak*, *Gathering of the Tribes*, and *Poetry Flash*. She currently lives in Maryland, where she is on the editorial board of the *Baltimore Review* and is Assistant Professor of English at the Community College of Baltimore County.

CURBSTONE PRESS, INC.

is a nonprofit publishing house dedicated to literature that reflects a commitment to social change, with an emphasis on contemporary writing from Latino, Latin American and Vietnamese cultures. Curbstone presents writers who give voice to the unheard in a language that goes beyond denunciation to celebrate, honor and teach. Curbstone builds bridges between its writers and the public – from inner-city to rural areas, colleges to community centers, children to adults. Curbstone seeks out the highest aesthetic expression of the dedication to human rights and intercultural understanding: poetry, testimonies, novels, stories, and children's books.

This mission requires more than just producing books. It requires ensuring that as many people as possible learn about these books and read them. To achieve this, a large portion of Curbstone's schedule is dedicated to arranging tours and programs for its authors, working with public school and university teachers to enrich curricula, reaching out to underserved audiences by donating books and conducting readings and community programs, and promoting discussion in the media. It is only through these combined efforts that literature can truly make a difference.

Curbstone Press, like all nonprofit presses, depends on the support of individuals, foundations, and government agencies to bring you, the reader, works of literary merit and social significance which might not find a place in profit-driven publishing channels, and to bring the authors and their books into communities across the country. Our sincere thanks to the many individuals, foundations, and government agencies who have recently supported this endeavor: Community Foundation of Northeast Connecticut, Connecticut Commission on Culture & Tourism, Connecticut Humanities Council, Greater Hartford Arts Council, Hartford Courant Foundation, Lannan Foundation, National Endowment for the Arts, and the United Way of the Capital Area.

Please help to support Curbstone's efforts to present the diverse voices and views that make our culture richer. Tax-deductible donations can be made by check or credit card to:
Curbstone Press, 321 Jackson Street, Willimantic, CT 06226
phone: (860) 423-5110   fax: (860) 423-9242
www.curbstone.org